ASHAMEFULLIFE

ASHAMEFULLIFE

Osamu Dazai

Translated from the Japanese
and with an Afterword by Mark Gibeau

Stone Bridge Press • *Berkeley, California*

Published by
Stone Bridge Press
P. O. Box 8208, Berkeley, CA 94707
tel 510-524-8732 • sbp@stonebridge.com • www.stonebridge.com

This publication has received the William F. Sibley Memorial Subvention Award for Japanese Translation from the University of Chicago Center for East Asian Studies Committee on Japanese Studies.

English translation © 2018 Mark Gibeau.

Originally published in Japanese as *Ningen shikkaku* in 1948.

Except on the cover and title page, Japanese names in this book appear as family-name first.

Cover design by Linda Ronan incorporating a photograph © Andrés Cañal Cañal. Text design by Peter Goodman.

Printed in the United States of America.

First digital print edition 2023.

p-ISBN: 978-1-61172-044-0
e-ISBN: 978-1-61172-932-0

CONTENTS

ASHAMEFULLIFE

PREFACE

I've seen three pictures of him.

The first is a photo of what I suppose might be called his childhood days and appears to have been taken when he was about ten years old. He stands at the edge of a garden pond, surrounded on all sides by a crowd of girls (his sisters and cousins, I imagine), dressed in rough-spun, striped *hakama* trousers, head tilted thirty degrees to the left and with a hideous grin on his face. Hideous? I suppose that the less perceptive (those with no training in aesthetics) might blandly say, "My, what a cute boy."

Empty praise perhaps, but the child's grinning face does possess a hint of what the vulgar call "cuteness," or at least enough of it to save the remark from crude flattery. Yet anyone with the least experience in aesthetic matters would but glance at the photo before thrusting it away in disgust as though it were a repulsive, hairy caterpillar, muttering, "What an odious child!"

Truly, the more I gaze at the boy's grinning face the more an inexplicable, disturbing sense of unease grows in me. Look there—it's *not* a smile. There isn't a trace of a smile on his face. The proof is in his hands, balled into tight fists. People don't smile with hands clenched in fists. It's a monkey. A monkey's grin. The face has simply been twisted into an ugly mass of wrinkles. The expression is so strange, so oddly deformed that I cannot help but recoil in revulsion. I'm tempted to call the figure

"Wrinkle Boy." Never in my life have I seen a child with such a peculiar expression.

The second photo also reveals a face that has undergone a surprising transformation. He is a student now. It isn't clear if the picture is from high school or university, but either way he is a startlingly beautiful youth. Yet, oddly, this photo also lacks the feel of a living, breathing person. Dressed in his school uniform, a handkerchief peeking from his breast pocket, he is relaxed, legs crossed as he leans back in a rattan chair, and, here too, he is smiling. This time it is not the grin of a wrinkled monkey but a finely crafted smile. Still, somehow, it differs from the smile of a human being. It lacks something. The quiet sobriety of life, perhaps, or the weight of blood. It lacks substance, possessing instead the lightness not of a bird, but of a feather. He is but a blank sheet of paper, smiling. From top to bottom everything feels contrived. This is not mere affectation—that falls far short of the mark. Nor is it just frivolity, flamboyance, or an attempt to appear charming. Clearly, he is not simply trying to appear fashionable. Yet, as I look at the photo more closely I experience a vague disquiet, as if I were reading a ghost story. Never in my life have I seen such a peculiar, beautiful young man.

The last photo is the most disturbing. I cannot guess his age. His hair is streaked here and there with gray. He sits in the corner of a filthy room (behind him the wall crumbles in three places), warming his hands over a small charcoal brazier. This time he is not smiling. His face is empty of all expression. It is as though he were already dead, even as he sits there with hands held over the brazier. An ominous, inauspicious photo. And that is not the only disturbing element of the picture. He sits so close to the camera that I can make out each element of his face in detail. He possesses an unremarkable brow, with unremarkable wrinkles. Unremarkable eyebrows, unremarkable eyes, unremarkable nose and chin. I give an exasperated sigh. His face isn't simply absent of expression, it fails to leave any impression at all. Nothing stands out. I gaze at the picture and then close my eyes. It's gone. I can see the walls and the small charcoal brazier but the face—the "protagonist" of the room—has vanished like mist in the sunlight, and, try though I might, I cannot bring it back. It is an unpaintable face, impossible even to caricature. Then, I open my eyes. I don't even feel the fleeting joy of recognition. There is no, "Ah, *that's* what he looked like!" To be perfectly blunt, I cannot remember what he looks like even as I stare at the photo with eyes wide open. There is only disgust, irritation, and the almost overpowering impulse to look away.

Even the face of someone slipping into death holds some kind of expression, leaves some kind of mark. But this, maybe this is what it would be like if the head of a carthorse were sewn onto a human body. In any case, a vague sense of revulsion shivers up my spine. Never in my life have I seen a man with such a peculiar face.

THE**FIRST**JOURNAL

I have lived a shameful life.

I can't understand how this thing called "human life" is supposed to work. I was born out in the country, in northeast Japan, so I was already fairly old by the time I saw my first steam engine. Back then I didn't realize that the bridges in the station were there simply to let people cross the tracks and get to their platform. I thought they were there to give the station an air of sophistication and fun—like a playground. I maintained this belief for quite some time, and clambering up and down those stairs always seemed to me the height of refined entertainment. Surely, I thought, this was the most considerate of all the services provided by the railroad. When I eventually discovered that they were nothing more than a practical set of stairs, my sense of delight vanished.

Another time, when I was a child, I saw an illustration of a subway. It never occurred to me that it might have been designed with some practical purpose in mind. I thought that people must have grown bored with riding above ground and the underground trains were built to provide new and exciting ways to travel.

I was a sickly child and often confined to my bed. I remember lying there, gazing at the sheets, the pillowcase, the quilt cover and so on, wondering at their insipid designs. It wasn't until I was nearly twenty years old that I realized that these things actually had a practical purpose, and, yet again, I was grieved by the dismal parsimony of humankind.

I never knew what it felt like to be hungry. No, I don't mean my family was so wealthy that I never wanted for the necessities in life—nothing so cliché as that. Rather, I mean I had absolutely no idea what the sensation of hunger felt like. I know it sounds strange, but even when I was hungry, I didn't know I was hungry. Whenever I got home from elementary or middle school, everyone would exclaim that I must be hungry, they remembered what it was like, they were always starving when they got back from school, and would I like some glazed beans? A bit of cake? Sweet buns? They made such a fuss that my inherent need to please others was roused and, muttering something about being hungry, I'd toss a handful of glazed beans into my mouth, but I never had the slightest inkling of what "hunger" was supposed to feel like.

Of course I eat—and I eat a lot—but I have almost no memory of eating out of hunger. I like to eat unusual dishes, delicacies. When I go out, I eat everything put before me, even if I have to force it down. That's why mealtimes at home were truly the most wretched moments of my childhood.

Ours was an old, country-style house, and at mealtimes the entire household—some ten people—formed two lines facing one another, a small tray set out before each person, and I, being the youngest, naturally sat at the very end of one of those lines in that gloomy dining room. The mere sight of my family, eating their lunch in silence, was enough to send shivers down my spine. Worse still, being a country household, we had the same thing every day. There were no unusual dishes, no delicacies, nor, indeed, any hope of them, so I came to live in terror of mealtimes.

Sitting at the very end of that gloomy row of trays, shivering in the cold as I picked up a few grains of rice at a time, shoving them into my mouth, I wondered why people felt compelled to sit down and eat three times a day, every single day. Everyone wore such solemn expressions as they ate that I began to entertain the notion that maybe this was all some kind of ritual. Perhaps, I thought, this was a sort of prayer—this act of gathering in the dreary dining room, all in a row, eyes downcast, three times a day, every day, always at the same time, trays lined up precisely, chewing food in silence whether we wanted it or not. Perhaps it was a ritual to placate the teeming spirits that filled the house.

When people told me I'd die if I didn't eat I thought they were just making mean threats. Still, that superstition (even now I can't help but think of it as such) filled me with dread. People die if they don't eat, so they work. They have to eat. Nothing seemed more impenetrable, incomprehensible, or menacing to me than this.

It seems that I will end my days having never understood anything at all about the lives of human beings. I fear my idea of happiness is completely at odds with everyone else's idea of happiness. This fear consumes me, sometimes making me twist and turn at night, groaning in agony, driving me to the brink of madness. Am I happy? Ever since I was a small child people have been telling me how fortunate I am, but, for my part, I felt like I was in hell, and the ones saying I was fortunate seemed incomparably and immeasurably happier than I was.

I was so miserable I sometimes thought I'd been afflicted with a dozen curses, any single one of which could crush the life out of a normal person.

In the end, I just don't understand. I cannot understand the kind or degree of suffering that other people experience. Perhaps their "practical" suffering, the kind relieved by eating, is in fact the most extreme form of suffering—perhaps it is a suffering so ghastly, like the tortures of the deepest circles of hell, that my "dozen curses" pale to insignificance beside it. I don't know. Yet, if that were the case, how do they endure it? How do they make it through each day without succumbing, without despairing, without committing suicide, even as they go on arguing about politics? Could they be such thoroughgoing egotists, so certain that this is the way things are supposed to be, that they have never once doubted themselves? If so, I suppose it might be easier to bear. I wonder if that is simply the way human beings are and that that is what makes them happy. I just don't know. . . . I wonder if they sleep soundly at night, if they awake refreshed in the morning. What do they dream about? What are they thinking about when they are walking down the street? Money? Surely that can't be the only thing. I recall someone saying that people live to eat, but I've never heard anyone say that people live for money. Yet, in the right circumstances . . . But, no, I don't understand that either. . . . The more I think about it, the less I understand and the more I find myself assailed by the terrifying, disquieting idea that I alone am utterly different. I can barely talk to people. I have no idea what to say or how to say it.

That's when I hit upon the idea of the clown.

It was to be my final attempt at courting humanity. Even though I lived in abject terror of people, I couldn't abandon them entirely. So I used the single, tenuous thread of the clown to retain my connection. On the surface, a grin never left my face, but on the inside I was locked in a desperate struggle, walking a tightrope, bathed in sweat, the danger of disaster ever imminent as I entertained them.

From the time I was a child I have had no conception of the suffering of others or what was going through their minds as they went about their lives, even among my own family. Terrified and unable to endure the relentless awkwardness of human interaction, I found that, without realizing it, I had transformed into an accomplished clown. Before I knew it, I had become a child incapable of uttering a single word of truth.

When I look at my family photographs from that time, everyone is wearing a somber expression, but I alone—without fail—have my face twisted into a peculiar grin. This is one example of my childish, pathetic clowning.

What's more, I never talked back when scolded by my parents, not even once. The smallest scolding seemed to me a deafening thunderclap, and it knocked me down with such tremendous force I thought I might go mad. Far from being able to talk back, such scoldings were like the pronouncement of some profound "Truth," echoing down the generations and across endless ages. Since I lacked the strength to embody that Truth, even at that age, I had already begun to suspect I might be incapable of living among humans. I was incapable of arguing with others, nor could I stand up for myself. If someone criticized me, my first thought was that the other person must be right, utterly and entirely, I must have made a terrible mistake, it couldn't be clearer. I endured such attacks in meek silence, but on the inside I writhed in agony, near mad with terror.

Of course, nobody likes being criticized and yelled at, but, in my case, I thought I glimpsed a terrifying animal nature in those angry faces—far more frightening and dreadful than any lion, crocodile, or dragon. Though usually concealed, a fit of rage might suddenly tear away the veil, just as a cow dozing idly in a pasture suddenly cracks its tail, obliterating a horsefly with a single blow. My hair stood on end and a shiver ran down my spine when I thought that possessing this instinct might be a necessary condition for living among humans. I came close to despair.

I lived in quivering terror of people, and, since I had no confidence whatsoever in my ability to speak or behave like a human being, I gathered up all of my fears and anxieties and concealed them in a box, deep inside my breast. I took enormous pains to conceal my melancholy and nervousness, and devoted myself instead to cultivating an air of innocent good cheer. Thus, little by little, I was transformed into an eccentric clown.

I would do anything so long as it made people laugh, it didn't matter what. If I could make them laugh, I reasoned, they might not care that I didn't really fit into their "lives." Above all else, I had to avoid sticking out. I had to avoid becoming an eyesore to those human beings. I am nothing, I am the wind, the sky. Such were my thoughts as I strove to entertain my family with my clowning. I played the clown—desperately— even for the maids and servants, as they seemed to me far more incomprehensible and terrifying than my own family.

Once, at the height of summer, I put a red woolen sweater on under my cotton robe and marched up and down the hallway, making everyone in the house laugh. Even my eldest brother, dour and rarely seen to smile, burst out laughing and, as though

he found the sight too delightful for words, called out to me saying, "Really, Yō-chan, I don't think that suits you."

What's that? I may have played the eccentric but I wasn't
such a fool that I couldn't tell hot from cold and I certainly
wasn't going to walk around in a wool sweater. I'd taken my sister's woolen leggings and, pulling them onto my arms, let the
ends peek out from my sleeves to make it look like I was wearing
a sweater.

My father was often away on business and kept a villa in the
Sakuragi district of Ueno, in Tokyo, where he spent the greater
part of each month. Whenever he came home he always brought
a mountain of presents for the whole family, even bringing some
for our distant relatives. I suppose it was a sort of hobby for him.

Once, before leaving for Tokyo, he gathered all of the children in the parlor and, smiling, asked each of us what we wanted,
writing the answers down in his notebook. It was rare for him to
be so intimate and friendly with us.

"And you, Yōzō?"

With that, I was struck dumb.

The moment I was asked what I wanted I ceased to want anything at all. What difference did it make? It's not as though anything could make me happy. At the same time, I was incapable
of saying no to anything offered me, no matter how little I might
desire it. I could not refuse anything, even if I didn't like it. If I
were being offered something I actually did want I could reach
for it only timidly, like a thief fearing discovery, a bitter taste in
my mouth as I writhed with indescribable terror. I lacked even
the ability to choose one thing over another. I suppose that this

failing was one of the causes of what was later to become my "life of shame."

I just stood there, squirming silently as Father grew irritated. "A book, I suppose? Or there's a place in Asakusa that sells lion masks, just like the ones in the New Year's lion dance—just the size for a child. Would you like one of them?"

The moment he asked, it was all over. I couldn't even come up with a silly response. My clowning had utterly failed me.

"You'd like a book, wouldn't you?" My eldest brother said, his expression ever serious.

"I see," Father said, exasperated. He closed the notebook with a loud snap, not bothering to write anything down.

What a disaster! I've made Father angry, his revenge will be terrible, I must do something right away, make amends before it's too late! Such were my thoughts as I lay trembling in bed that night. I slipped from under my blankets and snuck down to the parlor, where I slid open the drawer containing Father's notebook. Riffling through the pages until I found the list of presents, I licked the tip of a pencil and wrote "LION MASK" before sneaking back to bed. I didn't want the mask at all. On the contrary, I'd have preferred a book. But I knew that Father wanted to get me the mask and the whole purpose of this late-night adventure—this sneaking into the parlor and so on—was to ingratiate myself with him and to restore his good mood.

In the end, just as I expected, my extreme measures met with resounding success. When Father got back from Tokyo I heard his booming voice from my room, telling Mother all about it.

"So, I'm at the shop and I open my notebook, and there it was—see, right here! 'LION MASK.' Not my handwriting, either.

'What's this?' I think. I stood there trying to puzzle it out when it hit me. It's one of Yōzō's pranks! He just grinned and stood there like a lump but he must've wanted the mask so badly he couldn't help himself. He's an odd one, all right. Pretends he can't decide but then, there it is in black and white. If he wanted it so much all he had to do was say so. I burst out laughing right there in the shop! Call him down right away."

Another time I gathered all the maids and servants into our Western-style room and had one of the servants pound away on the piano (we may have been out in the country but we possessed all the accoutrements of a respectable household) as I ran around in circles, whooping in an Indian dance and making everyone laugh. One of my older brothers got his camera out and took a photograph of me. When the photo was developed you could see my tiny weenie peeking out from between the folds of the loincloth (I'd worn a thin, calico cloth typically used for wrapping packages) and this only served to bring the whole household down in gales of laughter yet again. I suppose that this too qualifies as one of my surprising successes.

In addition to the dozen or so monthly boy's magazines I subscribed to, I ordered various books from Tokyo that I read on my own. So I knew all the stories of "Professor Nonsense" and "Dr. Whatsit" and so on by heart. I also knew all sorts of ghost stories, transcriptions of famous storytellers, scary stories from old Edo, and more, all of which meant I was never lacking in material. I kept my family laughing by saying the most outrageous things with a perfectly straight face.

But oh, at school!

I was on the verge of being respected at school. The idea of being respected utterly terrified me. To me, "being respected" meant fooling everyone with a near-perfect deception until someone, some omniscient, omnipotent person saw right through me, crushing my façade into a handful of dust and condemning me to a shame worse than death. That was my definition of "respect." Even if I managed to deceive people and gain their "respect" eventually someone would find out and others would soon learn the truth. How terrible would their anger and revenge be once they realized they'd been duped? The mere thought of it made my hair stand on end.

I was in danger of being respected less because I came from a wealthy family than because I was, as they say, "brainy." I was a sickly child, so it wasn't unusual for me to miss a month or two of school at a time, confined to my bed. Once I missed nearly an entire year of classes. Yet, when the year came to an end I'd ride to school in a rickshaw and take my exams where, still weak from my illness, I'd score at the top of my class. Even when I wasn't sick I never studied and spent all my time in class drawing cartoons. I showed them to my classmates during recess, narrating as I went and making everyone roar with laughter. When we had to write compositions I always wrote funny stories, even when the teachers told me not to. I knew they secretly looked forward to them. One day I handed in a story, written in a tragic vein, about how I took a train to Tokyo with Mother and, mistaking the spittoon in the corridor for a chamber pot, peed in it by mistake. (I knew it was a spittoon all along. I only did it to make a show of my "childlike innocence.") Certain it would make the teacher laugh, I snuck out of the classroom as soon as he left and followed at a distance as he walked down the hallway. As soon as he was outside of the classroom he pulled my composition out from among my classmates' and, reading as he walked, began to chuckle. He stepped into the teachers' office and, no doubt having reached the end of the story, burst out laughing, tears streaming from his eyes. I saw him pass the story around to the other teachers. I could not have been more satisfied with the result.

A scamp.

I'd succeeded in presenting myself as a scamp. I had successfully avoided being respected. When grades came out I got ten out of ten in everything except "behavior," in which I received sixes or sevens. This too was a source of no small amusement at home.

My true nature, however, was very nearly the antithesis of a scamp. Young though I was, I had already been violated and exposed to the most desolate things by our maids and servants. To this day I maintain that performing such acts, on a small child, is the vilest, the crudest, and the cruelest crime that one human being can perpetrate on another. Yet I endured it. Sometimes I even laughed, weakly, thinking that in this I had discovered yet another of those "special qualities" peculiar to human beings. Had I been in the habit of telling the truth I might've gone to Mother or Father, without shame, telling them of these crimes and begging for their help. Yet even my own mother and father were incomprehensible to me. Appealing to human beings for help? The idea was laughable. Even had I appealed to Father, to Mother, to a policeman, to the government—wouldn't those people, adept as they were at getting their own way, just make up some story or other and that would be the end of the matter?

I knew all too well that I would never get a fair hearing. In the end, there was no use in appealing to others for help. All I could do, I thought, was to keep silent, to endure, and to persist with my clowning.

What's that you say? That I have no faith in people? Since when did I convert to Christianity? When did I start believing that all people are sinners? Perhaps some people will scorn me thus. But why should a lack of faith in humans lead you straight down the path to religion? Even the people who mock me, don't they live their lives happily, with never a thought for Jehovah or any deity, despite distrusting, and being distrusted by, everyone around them? This was also when I was very young, but one time a famous person from my father's political party came to town to give a speech and a group of servants took me to see it. The hall was packed and I saw a number of people who were particularly close to my father, all clapping with great enthusiasm. When it ended and the audience dispersed, each group made its own way home on the dark, snowy streets, and I heard them savagely criticizing the speech. Some of these voices belonged to Father's close friends. These so-called "allies" muttered angrily as they complained about Father's terrible introduction, that they hadn't been able to make heads nor tails of the speech. Then these very same people later came by our house and, stepping into our parlor, enthused over how successful the speech had been, their faces seemingly suffused with joy. Even the servants were guilty of this. When Mother asked them about the speech, they said it was fascinating. This, after spending the whole walk home complaining that there was nothing in the world so tedious as a speech.

This is but one example and an insignificant one at that. People spend their entire lives deceiving and lying to one another, yet, odder still, nobody seems especially offended by it. Human life is so full of pure, vivid, merry duplicity that I begin to think they don't even realize they are deceiving one another. For my part, I'm not particularly troubled by the deceptions. After all, what is my clowning but a lie I tell the whole day through? Questions of morality and the notions of right and wrong you find in ethics textbooks have never interested me. What I find incomprehensible are the people who can lead such pure, vivid, merry lives even as they lie to one another. Where do they get the confidence? Nobody has shared this secret with me. Had they done so perhaps I wouldn't have had to live in such terror of people, or to seek so desperately to please them. Perhaps I would've been able to avoid being excluded from the lives of human beings, perhaps I would've been able to live my life without tasting the hell of my nightly torments. In the end, it wasn't because of my distrust of others or because of Christianity that I was unable to seek help even when the servants inflicted their hateful crimes upon me. It was because human beings had sealed their hard shell of trust against me, against this "I" known as Yōzō. Even Mother and Father sometimes did things that were incomprehensible to me.

It seems to me that women have an instinctive ability to sniff out the scent of my isolation, my inability to appeal to others. That, I think, is one of the factors that led to me being taken advantage of at various times in later years.

To women, I was a man who could be trusted with the secret of their love.

THE **SECOND** JOURNAL

A score or more of towering, black-barked cherry trees lined the shore, so close to the water that the waves seemed to lap at their roots. At the start of the new school year their blossoms burst forth, a dazzling pink against the blue of the sea and the rust brown of sticky, newly sprouted leaves. The countless blossoms scattered in a blizzard of petals to form a heaving tapestry atop the surface of the sea, pulled away with each wave only to come crashing back to shore again. Despite neglecting my studies I had somehow managed to gain admittance to a middle school in Japan's northeast, and this petal-strewn beach was part of its grounds. The figure of these flowers blossomed on the badge of our school caps and even on each button of our uniforms.

One of the reasons Father chose this school of sea and cherry blossoms for me is that distant relations lived all but next door to it. I was left in their care. I was a lazy student in general and, living so close to the school, I always waited until the last minute before rushing off at the sound of the morning assembly bell. Even so, thanks to my clowning I grew more and more popular among my classmates with each passing day.

This was my first experience of living in an "unfamiliar land," and I decided that life in a foreign place was far easier than in one's own hometown. This might be put down to the fact that my clowning had by then become second nature and didn't require nearly so much effort. But I think it was due more to the gap in difficulty between performing for one's parents versus complete strangers, between one's hometown and a foreign place. Surely even the most gifted actors, even Jesus Christ the Son of God, was sensitive to that difference. Don't they say that the actor's most difficult stage is his hometown? Wouldn't even the most famous actor hesitate when confronted with a room filled with parents, siblings, wife, and children? Still, I managed it. What's more, my performances met with considerable success. Surely someone as cunning as I need not fear even the most unlikely of missteps in such a distant town.

My terror of people hadn't receded in the slightest—it may have even grown—and though fear still writhed deep in my breast I became so adept in my performances that I was forever making my classmates laugh. Even my homeroom teacher, who often complained about how much better the class would be if only I weren't in it, had to hide his grins behind his hand. I could even make the military drill instructor, with his barbaric shouting and voice like a thunderclap, collapse in laughter with the greatest of ease.

Just when I began to think I had finally managed to conceal my true nature entirely—just as I heaved a sigh of relief—to my utter astonishment I felt a knife pierce me from behind. The one doing the stabbing was, as you might expect, the scrawniest boy in the class. He had a pale, bloated face and wore baggy, hand-me-down robes that must have come from his father or an elder brother. The absurdly long sleeves made him look like Prince Shōtoku from an ancient scroll painting. He got terrible grades in all his classes and always sat on the sidelines during P.E. or military drill practice, and we naturally thought he was a bit simple. It never occurred to me that I should be on my guard even around him.

It was during P.E. and Takeichi (I can't remember his surname but I think his given name was something like Takeichi) was sitting on the sidelines as usual while we practiced the high bar. When it was my turn I deliberately arranged my face in a determined expression. I gave a great shout as I leapt but, instead of jumping up to grab the bar, I went straight ahead in a long jump, crashing down on my bottom with a thump in the sandpit. It was a completely planned failure. As I had intended, everyone burst out laughing, and I climbed to my feet, brushing the sand away with a sheepish grin. It was then that I felt a poke in my back and saw that it was Takeichi, suddenly standing behind me.

"Show off," he muttered.

I shuddered. That Takeichi, of all people, should see through me, see that my blundering was all an act—it was all too unexpected. For a moment I felt as though the whole world had turned red, that I burned in the crimson fires of hell. It was only with the greatest of effort that I managed to suppress the mad shriek welling up inside me.

The days that followed were filled with anxiety and terror.

On the surface, I continued to play the hapless clown, making everyone around me laugh, but from time to time a heavy sigh would escape as I realized that, no matter what I did, Takeichi had seen through me, and everything turned to ash. Certain that he would expose me to everyone who would listen, an oily sweat broke out across my brow and I glared about me, eyes rolling wildly with the vacant gaze of a madman. If I could have managed it, I would've spent every moment at Takeichi's side—watching him twenty-four hours a day to make sure he didn't let my secret slip. I would spare nothing to convince him that it was not an act, that my clowning was real. I wanted to become his dearest friend if I could. Should that fail, I thought, I would have no choice but to pray for his death. Yet, amid all of this, it never once occurred to me to actually try to kill him. Throughout my life I have wished more times than I can remember that someone might kill me, but I have never considered killing somebody else. Doing so, I thought, might only grant those terrifying people a measure of happiness.

In my quest to tame Takeichi I put on a "benevolent" grin, not unlike the smile of a fake Christian, and, head tilted to the left, I gently clasped his thin shoulder, inviting him to come to my house to play, my voice soothing, honeyed. He merely looked back at me in vacant silence. But then one day, near the start of summer I think, a sudden downpour turned the air white with rain just as classes ended, and everyone was milling about near the exit, wondering what to do. I lived just next door so the rain didn't bother me, and, just as I was about to make a run for it, I noticed Takeichi standing disconsolately in the shadows by the shoe locker. Come on, I'll lend you my umbrella, I grabbed his hand even as he flinched from me, pulling him out into the rain and running to my house. After asking my aunt to dry our jackets, I succeeded in getting Takeichi to visit my room on the second floor.

There were only three other people in the house. My aunt in

her fifties, her elder daughter, about thirty, wearing glasses, tall and sickly looking (apparently she'd been married once but had since returned home. I followed the others' example and called her Sis) and, lastly, the younger daughter called "Setchan," who had only just graduated from a women's college and who, unlike her sister, was short and round-faced. They ran a small shop on the first floor that sold stationery, balls, and bats and the like, but most of their money came from the rent on the five or six row houses that my aunt's late husband had left them.

"My ears hurt," Takeichi said, standing in the middle of my room. "They got wet and now they hurt."

Looking more closely, I saw that both of his ears were in a terrible state. They were so full of pus they looked ready to over-flow at any moment.

"Oh, how terrible!" I cried in exaggerated surprise. "That must really hurt!"

"I'm so sorry I pulled you out into the rain," I spoke ten-derly, in an almost womanly manner, as I made my "gentle" apology. I ran downstairs to fetch alcohol and cotton balls and made Takeichi rest his head on my lap as I carefully cleaned his ears. Not even Takeichi saw the evil intent behind this hypocrit-ical act. He even made an attempt at ignorant flattery as he lay there.

"You know, I bet girls will fall for you."

Many years later and to my regret, I was to discover that these words were a prediction. A prediction so terrible I doubt even Takeichi was aware of it. The words themselves are silly: to "fall for" someone, to have someone "fall for" you. Crude and absurdly foppish, no matter how ostensibly "austere" one's surroundings, their mere utterance is enough to cause the walls of even the most depressing temple to collapse before your eyes, leaving you feeling blank and empty. Yet it is a peculiar thing. If we move away from such crude notions as how difficult it is to have girls falling for you and instead, to phrase it in literary terms, consider the anxiety of being loved, then those depressing temple walls remain intact.

When Takeichi proffered this absurd flattery, saying that girls would fall for me, I just smiled and blushed as I cleaned his ears and did not say a word. Yet, in fact, I did have an inkling—if only faintly—that there might be something to what he said. Don't misunderstand me. I don't write "there might be something to what he said" in that absurd, self-satisfied, boastful sense that such uncouth expressions as "girls will fall for you" typically evoke. That would be too much, even coming from one of the dissolute young men who appear in *rakugo* stories. Clearly, I did not think, "there might be something to it" in this kind of ridiculous, smirking manner.

Women were a hundred times more difficult for me to understand than men. There were more women than men in my family and, even among my more distant relatives, there were many girls. There were also the maids who had "violated" me, and it is no exaggeration to say I grew up playing exclusively with girls. Yet, despite that, when I was with women I always behaved as though I were walking on thin ice. They seemed to me almost completely beyond understanding. I stumbled about blindly, sometimes accidentally treading on the tail of the tiger and suffering a terrible mauling as a result. Unlike the beatings I received at the hands of men, however, these wounds did not show. Like a kind of internal bleeding, they attacked me from the inside and in the most unpleasant manner imaginable. Such wounds were long and difficult to heal.

Women clasp me to them only to thrust me away. When others are around they scorn me and treat me cruelly, but the moment we are alone they cling to me. They sleep deeply, like the dead. I sometimes wonder if women live only to sleep. I'd made many observations about women, even when I was young. Though they were of the same species I could not help but think of women as altogether different from men, and, oddly, these enigmatic, mercurial creatures cared for me. To say that they "fell for me" or that they "loved me" would not, in my case, be accurate. It is more apt, I think, to say they "cared for me."

Women were even more at ease with my clowning than men. When I acted the clown around men, they did not, as you might imagine, cackle away, on and on and on. I knew that taking my performance too far around men would end in failure, so I was always careful to wrap things up at just the right moment. Women, though, do not understand moderation. They drove me on and on, demanding more and more of my clowning, calling for one encore after another until I was utterly exhausted. Women really do laugh a lot. They are capable of gorging themselves on pleasure much more than men.

When I was in middle school both the elder and the younger sister would visit my room on the second floor whenever they had a free moment. Each time I heard them at my door I jumped up in fright.

"Are you studying?" a tentative voice would ask.

"Nope," I'd reply, grinning as I closed my book. "Today, at

school, Gramps, he's our geography teacher . . ." and I'd make myself start rattling off another funny story.

"Yō-chan, put these glasses on," Setchan said one night, after she and Sis had come to my room and forced me to give one performance after another.

"Why?"

"Never mind why, just do it. Take Sis's glasses."

They were always ordering me about in this brusque manner. So the clown did as he was told and put on the glasses. The second I did so the two sisters burst out laughing.

"It's him! It's Lloyd! He looks just like him!"

Harold Lloyd, a foreign movie star known for his comedies, was very popular in Japan at the time.

I stood up, one hand raised.

"Ladies and gentleman," I began, "I would like to take this opportunity to tell all my fans in Japan . . ." This made them laugh all the harder and from then on I made sure to go to the theater whenever they screened a Lloyd film so I could secretly study his mannerisms and expressions.

Another time, I was lying in bed reading a book one autumn evening when Sis came flying into my room like a bird and threw herself onto my bed, collapsing in a fit of tears.

"Oh, Yō-chan, you'll save me, won't you? Of course you will! We should leave this wretched house—just the two of us. Oh, save me! Save me!"

She went on and on like this, raving and weeping in turn. This wasn't the first time I'd been exposed to a woman in such a state, so I wasn't terribly surprised at the violence of her words. On the contrary, I found her trite, empty theatrics rather tedious, and, slipping out from under my blankets, I walked over to my desk, peeled a persimmon, and handed her a slice. She sat up at this, sniffing and hiccoughing as she ate, and said, "Do you have any good books? Give me one."

I took down a copy of Sōseki's *I Am a Cat* and passed it to her.

"Thanks for the persimmon," she said with an embarrassed smile and walked out of the room. She wasn't the only woman who confused me. All women did. Trying to figure out what was going through their minds as they led their lives was more complicated, more troublesome, and more unsettling than trying to discern the thoughts of an earthworm. All I knew, as experience had taught me from a very young age, was that when a woman suddenly burst out crying like that, the best thing to do was give her something sweet. She'd start to feel better once she ate.

Sometimes the younger sister, Setchan, would even bring her friends to my room. As usual, I'd entertain one and all equally, but once they went home she invariably started criticizing them. You'd better watch out for that one, she's no good, she'd proclaim. In that case why go to all the trouble of bringing her up here? Thanks to Setchan, almost all of my visitors were women.

However, Takeichi's prediction, that women would "fall for me," had not yet been realized. I was still nothing more than northeastern Japan's Harold Lloyd. It would be several years yet before Takeichi's ignorant flattery came vividly to life, revealing itself as an ominous, disturbing foretelling.

Takeichi proffered one other, magnificent gift.

"Look! It's a monster!" He exclaimed when he came to my

room, proudly showing me a color print, the frontispiece of some book.

What's this, I thought. Years later I became convinced that it was in this precise instant that the path I later stumbled down was determined. I recognized the picture. It was merely Van Gogh's famous self-portrait. French impressionists were all the rage at the time, and, as art appreciation classes typically started off with these kinds of paintings, even middle school children in small country towns like mine could recognize works by Van Gogh, Cezanne, Renoir, and the rest. In my case, I'd seen many Van Gogh prints and been struck by his unique touch and his bright, vibrant colors, yet not once had it occurred to me to think of them as paintings of monsters.

"Well then, how about this one? Is this a monster, too?" I pulled a collection of Modigliani's paintings down from my bookshelf and showed Takeichi his famous portrait of a nude, her skin like burnt copper.

"Whoa!" Takeichi exclaimed, his eyes wide and round. "It looks like one of the horses of hell!"

"So it is a monster, then."

"I want to draw those kinds of monster pictures, too."

Contrary to what you might expect, just as timid and easily frightened people long all the more for a raging storm to grow stronger still, those who live in utter terror of human beings develop a psychological need to see, clearly and with their own two eyes, ever more frightening and terrible monsters but, alas, these artists, so wounded by that monster called humanity, are so terrorized that, in the end, they believe in visions, and monsters appear vividly before their eyes under the merciless glare of nature's noonday sun. What's more, they don't attempt clowning deceptions, they try to depict things precisely as they see them, resolutely drawing "monsters," just as Takeichi said. Here, I thought, are my future comrades, growing so flushed with excitement that hot tears trickled down my cheeks.

"I'll paint them, too. I'll paint monsters. I'll paint the horses of hell," I told Takeichi, my voice inexplicably dropping to a faint whisper.

Ever since elementary school I'd enjoyed both looking at pictures and painting my own. Yet my paintings never received as much attention as my written compositions. Since I placed no faith whatsoever in the language of human beings, my compositions were nothing more than a simple form of clowning. Throughout elementary and middle school they sent my teachers into paroxysms of laughter. But they meant nothing to me. It was only in my paintings (cartoons are a different story) that I struggled to express something in my own way, immature though it may have been. The model sketches from textbooks bored me, and the teacher's drawings were execrable, so I was left to my own devices, haphazardly cobbling together random styles of painting in an attempt to discover one for myself. By the time I started middle school I'd acquired a complete oil painting set, but though I tried to emulate the touch of the impressionists, my paintings always ended up looking flat and blank, the figures like paper dolls. I was at a loss. Thanks to Takeichi, however, I realized my approach had been completely wrong. In my naiveté and ignorance I'd taken things I thought were beautiful and tried to replicate that beauty in my paintings. True masters, however, took the most unremarkable objects and, through their own interpretation, created something beautiful. Or they took the ugliest objects and, through their unabashed fascination, imbued them with the joy of expression, even as the sight of them made their stomachs turn. In short, the true master is not swayed in the slightest by the expectations of others. It was Takeichi who bestowed this secret, this primitive treatise upon me, and, little by little, away from the eyes of my female visitors, I set myself to the task of composing self-portraits.

So dark and gloomy were these paintings that even I shrank from them. Yet, I told myself encouragingly, this is my true self, the one I so assiduously conceal in the depths of my heart. I smile cheerfully on the surface and make others laugh, but in truth mine is a melancholy soul. There was no point in denying it. Even so, I never showed my paintings to anyone other than Takeichi. I was afraid that people might see through my clowning and glimpse the misery it concealed, and I didn't want to be forced to be on my guard all the time. And I feared they might not realize that the paintings were an expression of my true self but rather see them as some new extension of my clowning and treat them as a hilarious joke. That would be far too much to bear, so I concealed my paintings in the deepest corner of my closet as soon as I finished them.

I also kept my "monster technique" secret at school. In art classes I continued to paint as before, with a mediocre touch, drawing beautiful things beautifully.

Takeichi was the only person I'd felt comfortable sharing my vulnerable, sensitive nature with, so I didn't worry about showing him my self-portraits. He praised them extravagantly, and when I had drawn two or three more monster paintings, he bestowed his second foretelling on me.

"You'll be a famous artist someday."

With these two predictions branded onto my forehead by poor, simple Takeichi—that girls would fall for me and that I'd someday become a famous artist—I soon made my way to Tokyo.

I'd rather have gone to art school, but Father had long since decided to send me to higher school with the aim of making me a government official. As usual, I was incapable of uttering a word of protest when this decision was handed down, and, without giving it much thought, I did as I was bid. I was told to give the entrance exam a try a year earlier than usual, and—being thoroughly sick of my school of sea and cherry blossoms—I passed the exam for a Tokyo higher school in my fourth year and so skipped my fifth year. I lived in a dormitory at first but was repulsed by its filth and brutality. There was no room for clowning in such a place, so, persuading a doctor to write a letter diagnosing me with pulmonary tuberculosis, I left the dormitory and moved into my father's Tokyo villa in Sakuragi. I could never live in a communal environment. Whenever I heard people going on about the "sincerity and enthusiasm of youth" or the "pride of youth" and that kind of thing I couldn't suppress a shudder. That kind of talk, that kind of "school spirit" was utterly alien to me. Classroom and dormitory alike seemed to me a midden heap of twisted sexual desire where my near-perfect clowning was of no avail.

When the Diet wasn't sitting Father only spent a week or two each month in Tokyo, and while he was away there were only three of us in the large house—me and the elderly couple who looked after the place—so I was able to skip classes now and then. Yet I never felt any desire to go out and see the sights of Tokyo (even now it seems I will end my days without ever having seen the Meiji Shrine or the bronze statue of Kusunoki Masahige or having visited the graves of the forty-seven samurai at Sengaku Temple) and instead spent the whole day at home reading and painting. When Father was in Tokyo I rushed off to class early each morning, but I sometimes stopped at Yasuda Shintarō's Western-style painting studio in the Sendagi district of Hongō instead, spending three or four hours at a time practicing my sketching. Ever since I'd escaped from the dormitory, even when I did show up to class I felt strangely distant from my classmates, as though I were just an auditing student. Perhaps this was a result of my own biases, but it became painfully obvious to me, and I grew increasingly reluctant to attend classes. Throughout my entire time at elementary, middle, and higher schools I never managed to understand what they meant by "school spirit." I never even bothered to learn any of my school songs.

Not long after I began frequenting the Yasuda studio an art student introduced me to the world of liquor, cigarettes, whores, pawnshops, and Marxism. An odd combination, to be sure, but it's true.

His name was Horiki Masao. Born in an older part of Tokyo, he was six years older than me and a graduate of a private fine arts academy. Since he didn't have an atelier at home, he visited the studio so he could continue his study of Western art.

"Hey, lend me five yen, will ya?"

I'd seen him around but we'd never spoken. Flustered, I thrust out a five-yen note.

"Excellent! You're a good kid. Let's have a drink—my treat."

Incapable of refusing, I let myself be dragged to a café district near the studio. That was the beginning of our acquaintance.

"Y'know, I've had my eye on you. For a while now. That! That shy smile, right there! That's the look of someone with the potential to be a real artist. To our new friendship, then—cheers! Hey Kinu, what do you make of this one? He's a pretty one, don't you think? Don't go falling for him, though. Since he started coming to the studio I'm only the second prettiest boy and more's the pity."

Horiki had a sallow complexion with sharp, chiseled features, and, unusual for an art student, he wore a suit, favored somber neckties, and parted his pomaded hair straight down the middle.

Unaccustomed to such places, I was in a constant state of terror. I kept crossing and uncrossing my arms, and, indeed, all I could manage was that shy smile. But after two or three glasses of beer, strangely, I began to experience a feeling of lightness, not unlike liberation.

"I wanted to go to art school but . . ."

"No, it's a bore. Boring! School is boring. Our teacher is nature herself! The pathos of nature!"

I didn't pay the slightest attention to his words. I thought he was a bit of an idiot, and no doubt his paintings would be terrible too. For all that, though, he might be a useful companion when it came to having fun. In short, for the very first time in my life, I'd met a real, live city scoundrel. Though we looked different—insofar as we were both cut off from the workings of this world of human beings, inasmuch as we were both confused— we were the same. The essential difference separating us was that, unlike me, his clowning was wholly unconscious and he was completely ignorant of its tragic nature.

We were just having fun. He was just someone to go out and have a good time with, I told myself. I scorned him and was even ashamed of our friendship sometimes as we walked about town together. Yet, in the end, I was destroyed even by the likes of him.

In the beginning, however, I thought him a fine fellow indeed. So fine a fellow one hardly saw his like, and, terrified of people though I was, even I was put off my guard as I found myself thinking I had discovered the perfect guide to Tokyo. To be honest, left to my own devices, I was even terrified of the conductors when I set foot on a train. I yearned to see a Kabuki play but was frightened of the young, female ushers who lined either side of the red carpet leading up the theater steps. At restaurants I was scared of the busboys, lurking silently behind me, waiting to clear my plate. And when it came time to pay the bill—oh, how I fumbled. I grew dizzy when it came time to hand over the money. My head spun, the world went dark, and I thought I was going half mad. Not out of parsimony, you see, but because I was so nervous, so embarrassed, so anxious and terrified. Far from trying to haggle the price down, not only would I often forget to take my change, it was so bad that I often even forgot to take the thing I had just purchased. It was utterly impossible for me to go walking about Tokyo on my own. That was the real reason I spent whole days lazing about at home.

When Horiki and I went out, I just handed him my wallet and let him do all of the haggling. He was quite adept at having fun. He could extract the greatest amount of pleasure from the smallest amount of money. We eschewed one-yen taxis, relying instead on his familiarity with the complex network of trains, buses, steamers, and every other cheap means of transport to get us to our destination in the shortest possible time. On the way home after a long night at the brothels he knew which inn to stop at for a bath, boiled tofu, and a quick drink—though cheap, it felt almost luxurious. He equipped me with a practical education. He extolled the virtues of *yakitori* and beef bowls as cheap and nutritious. He avowed that there was nothing better for getting drunk fast than an electric brandy cocktail. And when it came time to pay the reckoning, he never once gave me cause for anxiety.

Horiki's true value, however, lay in the fact that he never paid any attention to his listener's thoughts or feelings. He just went on and on, spouting his "pathos," with never a break in his banal chatter (perhaps that is the definition of "passion"—the ability to ignore the opinions of one's listener). When I was with Horiki there was never any danger that, exhausted from walking, we might lapse into one of those awkward silences. Whenever I was around others I was constantly on my guard in case one of those terrifying silences should suddenly appear. Though taciturn by nature, I felt obliged to press on with my clowning, desperately, as though some grand victory or terrible defeat hung in the balance. That fool Horiki, however, assumed the role of clown for himself without even realizing it, so I hardly ever had to speak at all. It was enough for me to smile from time to time and interject the occasional exclamation.

It didn't take me long to discover that liquor, cigarettes, and prostitutes were wonderfully effective ways to banish my fear of people, if only temporarily. It got to the point where I began to think that selling all I owned would not be too high a price to pay in order to continue these pursuits.

To me, prostitutes were neither human beings nor women but more like lunatics or idiots, and I could find solace in their embrace. I slept soundly when I was with them. They were so utterly lacking in anything like greed it was almost pitiable. Perhaps sensing a kindred spirit, they displayed a natural, though not oppressive, affection toward me. Theirs was an affection free from calculation, an affection devoid of ulterior motives, the affection you feel for a person you might never meet again. Some nights I actually saw the Madonna's halo hovering over their heads, those idiots and lunatics.

Yet, while I visited the brothels in search of some meager respite from my terror of humanity—if only for a night—and as I entertained myself with my kindred spirits, I started to undergo an unexpected change. An inauspicious aura began to coalesce about me, eddying and swirling. It was, I suppose, a kind of "gift" that prostitutes bestowed on a favored customer, though not one I had expected to receive. The contours of this gift gradually became visible and grew increasingly distinct so that, when Horiki finally pointed it out to me, I was both astonished and, I must admit, disgusted. To put it in objective though somewhat vulgar terms, the whores had been training me. They had been teaching me how to interact with women. Worse still, being prostitutes, they were relentless when it came to the study of this particular field, and their training had already effected quite a change in me. I'd become quite the adept. Already, it seemed, I'd acquired the scent of a "Don Juan" and women (not just whores) seemed to pick up on it instinctively, converging on me. This lascivious and disreputable air, it seems, was the "gift" they'd granted me, and that gift, more than my pursuit of respite, was starting to attract an uncomfortable amount of attention.

Horiki probably intended the remark as a compliment, at least in part. Yet I couldn't help but feel something disturbing and oppressive in it. For example, there was the naive, childish letter sent by a woman at a café. There was the general's daughter of about twenty who lived next door to me in Sakuragi; each morning around the time I left for school, she would be loitering near her gate, wearing makeup, for no apparent reason. There was the time I went to a steakhouse and one of the maids—though I hadn't so much as said a word to her . . . And when I bought cigarettes at the local tobacconist's, inside the box she handed me . . . The woman sitting next to me at the Kabuki play . . . The night I got drunk and fell asleep on the train . . . When, completely out of the blue, I received a brooding letter from the daughter of a relative back home . . . Or when a girl—I have no idea who—left a handmade doll for me at my house when I was out. I am extraordinarily passive, so none of these incidents developed into anything more, they were mere fragments, yet it's difficult to deny that some kind of aura seemed to linger about me, ensnaring women. I'm not joking or boasting of my romantic prowess—it is simply the truth. But that someone like Horiki should point it out to me caused a pain not unlike humiliation, and with that my desire to seek the company of prostitutes cooled markedly.

One day, perhaps thinking to appear fashionably modern (being Horiki, it is difficult to imagine any other reason), Horiki took me to a secret gathering, a kind of communist reading group (I think they called it the "R-S" but my memory is vague). For Horiki, this kind of thing was no doubt nothing more than another stop on his "grand tour of Tokyo." I was introduced to the "comrades," forced to buy some pamphlets, and then subjected to a lecture on Marxist economics by the leader of the group, a young man with a profoundly ugly face. I couldn't help but think that everything they said was nothing more than common sense. It was true enough, but there is more to the human soul than just that. There is also something incomprehensible, something terrifying. Desire is too weak a word for it, as is vanity. Even if we combine Eros and desire it's still not quite enough. I'm not sure myself what it is, but I am certain that the foundation of human society is not economics. It's something more, with the uncanny air of a strange and scary folk tale. Living in abject terror of that strange folk tale as I did, I was able to accept theories of materialism as easily as I accepted the fact that water runs downhill, but these theories did not liberate me from my dread of humans, they did not arouse in me a sense of joy or the hopefulness of a man whose eyes have been opened to the newly sprouted, green leaves of spring. Nevertheless, I attended every single meeting of the "R-S" (again, I think that was the name but I may be mistaken). It was all I could do not to burst out laughing at their debates. They were all so tense and grave as they became engrossed in their absurd, obvious attempts to demonstrate the theoretical equivalent of one and one making, in fact, two. I used my clowning to try to make the meetings a bit more relaxed, and, perhaps as a result, the atmosphere did grow a bit less stuffy. I was soon so popular I'd become an indispensable member of the group. These naive people must have taken me for one of their own, a naive youth like them. A happy-go-lucky, clowning "comrade." If so, they were deceived from start to finish. I was not their comrade. Still, I attended every meeting without fail, entertaining all with my antics.

I went because I liked it. Because I was fond of the people. That is not to say, however, that our intimacy was born out of our mutual devotion to Marxism.

"Illicit." It aroused a faint thrill in me. Or rather, I found the concept almost comforting. For it was the legitimate parts of the world that terrified me (I sensed in them something infinitely strong). Their workings mystified me, and I couldn't endure sitting in that freezing, windowless room. Though the outside might be nothing but an ocean of lawlessness I thought it better by far to dive in and swim until I should die.

There is a word: "pariah." In human society this word is used to indicate those who have failed, the pathetic, the immoral. Ever since I was born, I felt I was a pariah, and whenever I met someone that society had also deemed worthy of being so branded I always felt a deep sense of compassion. So deep was my compassion that I sometimes caught myself in silent admiration of it.

There is another phrase: "guilty conscience." I've lived my whole life plagued by my conscience yet, at the same time, it has been a faithful companion—like a devoted wife standing by me through thick and thin as the two of us frolic in our gloom. There's also the saying "to have skeletons in one's closet." For me, those skeletons appeared the moment I was born, and, instead of disappearing as I grew up, they became stronger and more solid until they weighed so heavily upon me that I suffered the torments of a million different hells each night. Even so (no doubt this will sound very odd), they gradually came to be more familiar to me than my own flesh and blood. Their weight, like the pain of an open wound, was like whispered protestations of love. To such a man as me, the mood of the underground political meetings I attended was thus strangely relaxing and oddly comfortable. In the end, it wasn't the movement's goals but its nature that attracted me. The only reason Horiki went was to mock them as a bunch of idiots, and, after the initial introduction, he never returned. Their mission might be to research production, he would say, but mine is to research consumption, and, with that lame jest, he never went back, henceforth inviting me only to participate in his research of consumption. Now that I think back on it, I see there were several different kinds of Marxists. Some were like Horiki, people who became self-proclaimed Marxists in a pique of vain modernity, and then there were those like me who, drawn by the scent of the illicit, merely settled themselves in their midst. Had the true believers among the Marxists ever guessed at our real natures I don't doubt that their anger would have been as a raging inferno. They would have condemned us as contemptible traitors and expelled us on the spot. Yet neither I nor even Horiki were ever expelled. I, especially, felt more relaxed and was able to behave in a "healthier" manner in that illicit, underground world than I could among the gentlemen of polite society, and it wasn't long before the others came to see me as a promising young "comrade," entrusting me with all sorts of tasks, each enshrouded in such an absurd degree of secrecy that it was difficult not to laugh. What's more, I never refused any task, I accepted all with equanimity, I never got rattled or attracted the suspicion of the "dogs" (that's what the comrades called the police). I never blundered or did anything that would get me taken in for questioning. Laughingly—and making everyone else laugh—I undertook all kinds of dangerous missions (members of the movement would grow terribly tense, as if they were attempting something of monumental importance. Like in a second-rate detective novel, they used such extreme caution in the execution of tasks so insignificant I could not help but feel a bit bewildered by it all. Nevertheless, when it came to making my errands sound perilous, they spared no effort), or so they called them, without flaw or mishap. At the time, the prospect of being arrested as a party member and imprisoned, even if it was for life, didn't trouble me in the slightest. Compared to the terror I felt toward "real life" in human society and the hellish torments of my nightly insomnia, I sometimes thought that life in prison might be an improvement.

Though Father and I lived in the same house, between his visitors and his going out it wasn't unusual for us to go three or four days without seeing one another. Still, his was a formidable, terrifying presence and I contemplated moving out—perhaps to some sort of boarding house—but even as I tried to muster up the courage to discuss it, the old caretaker informed me that Father was planning to sell off the house.

Father's term of office was coming to an end and, no doubt having his own reasons for it, he'd decided not to stand for re-election. He'd drawn up plans to add a new wing to our estate at home as a retreat for his retirement and, not having any remaining ties to Tokyo, he must've thought it wasteful to maintain an entire house, complete with servants, for the sake of a mere student

(Father's mind, like the minds of everyone else in human society, was a mystery to me). So the house soon passed into the hands of another, and I moved into a gloomy room in a boarding house called "The Hermitage" in the nearby Hongō district, where I immediately found myself struggling to make ends meet.

Before, I'd been receiving a monthly allowance from Father, and, even if I spent it all in two or three days, there were always cigarettes, liquor, cheese, fruit, and so on to be had around the house. When it came to things like stationery, books, and clothes I could go to any of the local shops and put them on my father's account. If Horiki and I went out for noodles or a tempura rice bowl, I had only to go to one of the restaurants my father patronized. I could leave without paying and nobody said a word.

Now, suddenly living on my own at the boarding house, I had to make do with the allowance alone. I was at a complete loss. Naturally, my money vanished in two or three days. I was horrified, and, growing so wretched that I thought I might go mad, I sent telegram after telegram to Father, to my brothers and my sisters in turn, begging them to send money, saying I would explain in a letter to follow (the circumstances I explained in those letters were, each and every one, mere empty clowning. I thought that if I was going to ask for something I should at least try to make them laugh). Under Horiki's tutelage I diligently commuted to and from the pawnshops yet, even so, I was forever short of funds.

In the end, I simply didn't possess the ability to make it on my own, alone in a boarding house without any connections to help me. I was too frightened to simply stay at home. I would be overcome by the fear that a complete stranger might burst in at any moment and attack me, so, as though dodging a blow,

I fled into the city, helping out in the movement or drinking at cheap bars with Horiki. I'd all but abandoned my studies and my painting and, in November of my second year of school, I became embroiled in a love suicide with an older, married woman, and my life changed forever.

I skipped all my classes and never studied for any of my subjects, but I seemed to have an odd knack for exams so, one way or another, I was able to maintain the deception with my parents. However, unbeknownst to me, the school had contacted my parents directly, telling them that I would soon surpass the limit for absenteeism. Soon, at Father's direction, my eldest brother started sending me long letters full of stern warnings. Yet, what really troubled me—far more than school—was my lack of funds and the fact that my work for the movement had gotten so demanding I could no longer treat it as a joke. I'd been promoted to the head of the Marxist Student Corps for the Central District or something like that. In any case, I was in charge of Hongō, Koishikawa, Shitaya, Kanda, and all the surrounding areas. People started talking about an armed uprising, so I bought a small pocketknife (thinking back on it, it was such a flimsy thing I doubt it would've served to sharpen a pencil) and took to carrying it about in the pocket of my raincoat as I ran about town making "contacts." All I wanted to do was get drunk and sleep like the dead, but I didn't have any money. And the "P" (that was our code word for the party. Or at least I think it was—I may be mistaken) kept sending me out on mission after mission, never giving me enough time to catch my breath. Given my delicate health it was highly unlikely I'd be able to keep it up for much longer. I'd only started in the movement because I was attracted to the "illicit," so I couldn't help feeling annoyed when it began to occupy so much of my time. Privately, I came to the conclusion they'd picked the wrong person for the job and should give it to one of their true believers instead. So I ran away. As you might expect, that didn't make me feel very good, and I resolved to die.

At the time, there were three women who were particularly fond of me. One was the boarding-house owner's daughter. After I got home at night, bone-tired from my work for the movement, heading straight to bed without even bothering to eat, she would invariably come knocking at my door saying, "I'm sorry but my brother and sister are making so much noise downstairs that I can't concentrate on this letter." And with that she'd settle herself at my desk to write for an hour or more.

It wouldn't have been so bad if I could have just ignored her and gone to sleep but it was obvious she wanted me to talk to her, and, as usual, this sparked my passive need to please. Worn out as I was, I wasn't interested in exchanging so much as a single word with her, yet, even so, I gathered up my remaining energy and, rolling over onto my stomach, lit a cigarette, saying, "I hear there's a man who heats his bath with the love letters he gets."

"That's horrid! Talking about yourself, I suppose?"

"I did warm up some milk once."

"My, my, what an honor. Drink up, then."

I just wanted her to hurry up and leave. The whole pretense of the letter was a joke. I was certain she was just scribbling nonsense.

"Show me," I said, though I'd sooner die than read it. What? No! No, you mustn't, she protested with obvious delight. It was so terribly pathetic that any interest I might've had quickly vanished. Then I got the idea of sending her on an errand.

"Hey, I'm really sorry but can you do me a favor? There's a pharmacy down on the avenue by the streetcars—can you pick up some Carmotine for me? I'm so exhausted I'm burning up, and I'm so tired I can't even sleep. Would you mind? The money . . ."

"Oh, don't worry about the money," she said, jumping happily to her feet. As I knew very well, women are delighted when a man asks them to do something for him, it is never a cause for distress.

The second woman was one of my "comrades" who studied in the humanities at a women's teacher's college. Since we were both involved in the movement I saw her every day, whether I wanted to or not. Even after the meetings finished she would follow me around for hours on end and was always buying me all sorts of presents.

"You can think of me as your elder sister."

Though this crude affectation made me shudder I could only reply, "Of course I will," forcing my face into a faint, melancholy smile. I mustn't make her angry, I thought, frightened. I had to distract her somehow. I became so focused on placating this ugly, disagreeable woman that I soon found myself entertaining her. I tried to make her laugh with my jokes, and when she bought me presents (they were always in the worst possible taste, and I gave most of them away to people like the old man running the *yakitori* stall) I forced myself to feign delight. One summer night when she simply wouldn't leave me alone, I led her into a dark alley and kissed her in the hope it would make her go home. Instead, she grew wild with excitement, and, overcome by a crude madness, hailed a taxi to take us to one of the tiny offices the movement rented secretly, where we raised quite the racket until dawn. I smiled wryly as I wondered just what kind of elder sister she thought herself to be.

Along with the girl at my boarding house, I had no choice but to see this "comrade" every day, and, unlike the other women I'd known, there was no way to avoid them. Before long my usual anxiety took over, and I was running myself ragged in my attempts to keep the both of them happy. I felt trapped, unable to move so much as a finger.

Around the same time one of the waitresses at a large Ginza café did me an unexpected favor. Though I'd only met her the one time, I couldn't dispel my sense of obligation, so, again I found myself all but paralyzed with worry and imagined fears. I'd learned by then to affect sufficient impudence that I no longer needed Horiki to guide me about town. I could take the train on my own, go to Kabuki plays, and even walk into cafés, dressed though I was in cheap, threadbare clothes. On the inside, of course, I was the same as I'd always been, and the suspicion, terror, and anxiety I felt toward the violence and confidence of human beings was undiminished. Only on the surface had I slowly reached the point where I could greet people with a straight face. Well, no, that's not precisely true. I invariably employed the wry grin of a defeated clown, but, regardless, though my greetings and small talk might be hopelessly confused, I'd nevertheless managed to cultivate a "talent" for it. Was it thanks to my work with the movement? Or was it women? Or liquor? The main reason I was starting to acquire these new skills, I suspect, is that I was broke. This induced in me a state of constant terror no matter where I was, and I thought the sense of oppression might ease somewhat if I immersed myself in the jostling crowd of drunks, waitresses, and busboys typical of big cafés. So it was that, with ten yen in my pocket, I went alone to a Ginza café and, grinning at the waitress, said, "I've only got ten yen, so don't expect much."

"Don't worry."

She spoke with a faint Kansai accent. And, oddly, her simple words soothed my jangling nerves. No, not because I didn't have to worry about money; it was because I got the sense that I didn't have to worry about being with her.

I drank. I felt relaxed around her, and, not feeling compelled to play the clown, I let my true nature show through, drinking in gloomy, taciturn silence.

"Would you like any of these?" she asked, laying a variety of dishes out on the table. I just shook my head.

"Just liquor? I'll join you, then."

It was a cold, autumn night. At Tsuneko's request (I think that's what she called herself but my memory has faded so I can't be sure. That says a lot about the kind of person I am. I even forget the name of the person I tried to commit suicide with), I went to a sushi stall in one of the alleys of Ginza and, eating truly terrible sushi (though I can't recall her name, the sushi—or rather, how bad it was—remains firmly fixed in my memory. I remember the old man running the stand had a crew cut and a face like a Japanese rat snake. He made a show of flailing about as he made the sushi, pretending he actually knew what he was doing. I can see all of this as clearly as if it were right before me. Years later and more than a few times I have caught myself looking at a face that seems oddly familiar before realizing, with a wry smile, that it looks like that old man from the sushi stand. Though the woman's name and, by now, even her face have faded from my mind, the fact that I can still recall that old man's face so clearly I could draw it from memory shows how bad the sushi was and how cold and miserable it made me feel. In any case, though I've been taken to supposedly famous sushi restaurants, I've never enjoyed sushi. The pieces are too big. Why couldn't they just make them smaller? Why not just make them thumb-sized?), I waited for her to finish her shift.

She lived in a rented room over a carpenter's workshop in Honjo. I made no effort to conceal my gloomy nature as I sat in her room, drinking tea, one hand pressed to my cheek, as though I had a terrible toothache. Oddly, rather than being repelled, she seemed drawn to this attitude of mine. She too seemed utterly alone. A cold, early winter wind blew about her, with only dead leaves whirling crazily about her.

As we lay there she told me she was two years older than me, from Hiroshima . . . I have a husband, he was a barber back in Hiroshima but we ran off, came to Tokyo last spring, he never bothered with a proper job after that, he got arrested for fraud, he's in prison now, I visit him every day, I bring him all sorts of gifts, starting tomorrow I'm not going back. On and on she went, telling me the story of her life. I'm not sure why but I always get bored when women start telling me about their lives. Maybe it's because they aren't very good storytellers—they emphasize all the wrong parts—but it all goes in one ear and out the other.

Forlorn.

Had a woman but whispered that one word it would have evoked more sympathy from me than the thousands and millions of other words they expended talking about themselves. It seems strange and almost mysterious that I've never heard a woman speak that one word. Though Tsuneko never uttered the word "forlorn" aloud, it seemed to eddy about her, like a current of air an inch thick, and when I was near, it enveloped me as well, blending and merging perfectly with my own stinging current of melancholy. Just as "The autumn leaf settles on a stone in water's depths," I was able to distance myself from my fear and my anxiety.

The night I spent with this wife of a man imprisoned for fraud was, for me, joyous (I doubt I will again so unhesitatingly employ such bold and positive language in the entirety of my journals) and liberating in a manner completely different from the deep, peaceful sleep I found in the arms of those simple-minded prostitutes (who were nothing if not cheerful).

Yet, it was only the one night. When I woke in the morning, I jumped up and once again dressed myself in the guise of the frivolous clown. The true coward is frightened even by happiness. He is bruised even by cotton wool. He is wounded even by joy. Panicking, I wanted to escape, quickly, before I got hurt, so I surrounded myself in the familiar smoke screen of the clown.

"You know that old saying? 'Love flies out by the window when poverty comes in by the door'? Most people have it all wrong. It doesn't mean the woman leaves when the man runs out of money. It's, when a man runs out of money he . . . he loses heart, he's no good. He gets so weak he can't even laugh, he gets this strange inferiority complex, he gets desperate, and he's the one who pushes the woman away. At that point he's half mad and he starts pushing and shoving and shoving until he breaks free.

Well, at least that's what it says in a book I read. Sad, isn't it? Alas, I know the feeling all too well."

I seem to recall saying something stupid along those lines, making Tsuneko burst out laughing. "Well, there's no point in dawdling," I said, and with a "thanks for everything," I left without so much as washing my face. My silly story about "love flying out when poverty comes in" created unexpected complications later.

A month or so went by before I saw my benefactor of that evening again. With each passing day the joy I had experienced faded and the fleeting kindness she'd shown filled me with a growing sense of dread. Even the most mundane things, such as when Tsuneko paid my bill at the café, aroused in me a terrible sense of obligation, and this came to distress me more and more. Before long I started thinking of Tsuneko much as I thought of the girl from my boarding house or the "comrade" from the women's teacher's college. I came to see her only as a threat and, though she was far away, I lived in constant terror of her. To make things worse I couldn't help thinking that, should I run into a woman I'd once slept with, she would suddenly explode in a furious rage. The prospect of meeting my former lover was thus extremely disagreeable to me, and I kept a respectful distance from Ginza. Now, this attitude of mine was not born of cunning but from the simple fact that I had yet to come to terms with one of the stranger aspects of women. I could not comprehend how a woman could sleep with me and then wake up the next morning as though her memory had been wiped clean and, in the most splendid manner, go on with her life as if the world of night and the world of day were completely cut off from one another.

Toward the end of November Horiki and I were drinking at a cheap stand bar on the side of the road in Kanda. When we left, my disreputable friend insisted we go somewhere else and keep drinking. Let's drink, let's drink, he kept saying over and over again, although neither of us had any money. I was fairly drunk by this point and, feeling particularly daring, said, "All right, then. I'll take you to the land of dreams. Prepare yourself! I'll take you to a feast, to lakes of liquor, to forests of food. . . ."

"A café?"

"Yup."

"Let's go!"

And with that we hopped on a streetcar. Horiki, in high spirits, announced, "I'm starving for a woman! Can I kiss the waitress?"

Horiki knew that I disliked it when he played the vulgar drunk, so he persisted, trying to gain my permission.

"I'm really going to do it. You wait and see—whoever sits next to me, I'm going to kiss her. You'll see!"

"Do what you like."

"You are too kind. I'm starving for a woman."

We got off at Ginza 4-chōme and, putting all our faith in Tsuneko's generosity, walked into that massive café, that veritable lake of liquor and forest of food despite not having a single coin between us. We stopped at the first empty booth we saw, and Horiki and I sat down facing one another. Tsuneko and another waitress came running up to us. The other woman sat next to me. I let out a faint gasp when Tsuneko dropped down next to Horiki. She was about to be kissed.

I didn't feel any regret. I wasn't a particularly possessive person and, even should I feel the occasional glimmer of jealousy, I lacked the spirit to fight for my claim. So much so that, later, I would even stand and, without a single word of protest, watch my common-law wife being violated.

I wanted to keep as far away from the squabbling of human beings as I could. I was terrified of being drawn into that maelstrom. My relationship with Tsuneko had been limited to that one night. She didn't belong to me. There was no reason for me to feel regret or any other kind of arrogant desire. Nevertheless, I gasped.

It was a gasp of pity, of pity for poor Tsuneko, about to be roughly kissed by Horiki, right in front of me. Defiled by Horiki, she would no doubt feel obliged to break with me and I, I lacked the necessary passion to stop her. Though I gasped at that moment, at Tsuneko's misfortune, thinking that everything was over now, I was also filled with a sense of resignation, as pure as water, and I smirked as I looked from Horiki to Tsuneko and back again.

To my surprise, however, things turned out much worse than I expected.

"I can't!" Horiki exclaimed, his mouth twisting. "Not even I could kiss such a dreary woman." He grimaced, as though at a complete loss, and, arms crossed, he stared at Tsuneko.

"Bring us something to drink. We don't have any money," I muttered to Tsuneko. In truth, I wanted to drown myself in liquor. In the eyes of a philistine, Tsuneko might be nothing but a glum, penniless woman, not even worth the kiss of a lecherous drunk. This thought hit me, unexpectedly and unintentionally, like a thunderclap. That night I drank and I drank, I drank more than I'd ever drunk before. I drank until I could barely stand. Tsuneko and I gazed into one another's eyes, smiling sadly. No, there was no denying it. She was an oddly frayed woman, she reeked of poverty. And yet, even as I thought this, I felt an affinity with her, the affinity of one poor person for another (I am convinced that, hackneyed though it may be, the fundamental incompatibility of the rich and the poor remains one of the great, timeless dramatic themes), and that, that intimacy, filled my heart. A fondness for her began to grow in me and, for the first time in my life, I sensed the stirrings of what was, for me, a passionate, though somewhat feeble, love. I vomited. I can't remember anything before or after that point. It was the first time I'd drunk so much that I completely lost myself.

When I awoke Tsuneko was sitting beside my pillow. I was in her room above the carpenter's shop.

"I thought you were joking, all that talk about love flying out when poverty comes in, but you were serious, weren't you? You never came back. Not a very clean break, though, was it? What if I make enough for the both of us? Would that work?"

"No."

Then she lay down next to me. It was around dawn when she first spoke of death. It seemed that she too was weary of living the life of a human being and, for my part, when I thought of my own terror of the world, with all its complications, of money, of the movement, of women, of school—I didn't see how I could possibly go on. So I blithely assented to her plan.

None of it seemed real to me at the time, though. The true import of her words, "let's die," had escaped me. They seemed to conceal an element of "play."

Later that morning we were wandering around the sixth ward of Asakusa. We went to a coffee shop and I drank a glass of milk.

"Can you get the bill?"

I stood and, taking my coin purse from the sleeve of my kimono, I discovered that I had only three copper coins. I was assailed not so much by shame as by horror. Instantly the desolate scene of my room at the boarding house appeared before my eyes, nothing but a bed and my school uniform. Not a single item left to be pawned, my only other possessions the clothes on my back. This is my life. The realization forced itself on me. I could not go on.

Seeing my confusion, Tsuneko stood up and peered into my purse.

"Oh, is that all you've got?"

She spoke innocently enough, yet even so, pain pierced me to the bone. It was the first time that the mere voice of someone I loved caused me pain. Whether or not it was all I had didn't matter. Those three coins weren't money. They were a special kind of humiliation, one I'd never tasted before. An unendurable humiliation. I suppose that I hadn't yet managed to get away from thinking of myself as a "rich boy." At that moment, now fully aware of what it meant, I resolved to seek my own death.

That night, the two of us jumped into the sea at Kamakura. I borrowed this from a friend at the café, she said, unwinding her *obi,* and, folding it carefully, she placed it on a boulder. I took off my cloak, lay it next to the *obi,* and we leapt into the sea.

The woman died. I alone was saved.

Being a higher school student and, perhaps because Father's

name possessed some measure of what they call "news value," the incident was splashed all over the papers and became quite the scandal.

I was admitted to a hospital by the sea, and one of my relatives from home rushed down to handle all of the arrangements. Before he left he told me that everyone at home—Father first and foremost—was furious with me and that I'd be lucky not to be disowned. I didn't care about any of that, though. I missed Tsuneko and couldn't stop weeping at the thought of her. Of all the people I'd known, poor, threadbare Tsuneko was the only one I'd truly loved.

I received a long letter from the girl at my boarding house, a composition of fifty poems, each beginning with the peculiar phrase, "Live for me!" Fifty. The nurses too were always stopping by to see me, smiling brightly. Some of them even took my hand, squeezing it tightly as they left.

It was then that they discovered an abnormality in my left lung. This was a wonderfully convenient turn of events for me, as, when the police eventually came and took me in for the crime of abetting suicide, they treated me as an invalid and put me in a special holding cell apart from the others.

Later the night of my arrest, the old policeman standing the night watch in the guard's quarters next to my cell came over and slid the door open quietly.

"Hey," he said, calling out to me. "You must be freezing in there. Come on over here—sit by the fire."

I made a show of shuffling dejectedly out of my cell and into the guardroom, and sat on a chair next to the charcoal brazier.

"You really miss her, don't you, the girl who died?"

"Yes." So faint were my words they seemed to vanish.

"Well, that's love, isn't it?" The guard was working himself up to something.

"So, where did you first establish relations with her?" He began questioning me, acting for all the world like an officer of the court. He spoke condescendingly, as though I were a mere child and he the chief prosecutor in charge of the investigation. In the end, his real motive was simply to while away the tedium of a long autumn night by getting me to recount all the salacious details. I saw through him at once, and it was hard not to laugh. Of course, I knew I was under no obligation to answer any of the questions in his "unofficial interrogation," but I went along with his charade to add a bit of spice to the dull evening. I acted like I believed, beyond any shadow of a doubt, that he was no less a figure than the chief investigator himself and that my fate lay wholly in his hands. I made up one absurd "statement" after another, all intended to more or less satisfy his prurient curiosity.

"Yes, I see now. I think I understand the situation. You know, we take it into account when people are forthcoming and answer all of our questions honestly."

"Thank you very much. I am in your debt."

I have to say mine was a masterful performance. An impassioned performance that did not stand to benefit me in the slightest.

When morning came I was summoned to the chief's office. Now it was time for the official interrogation.

The moment I opened the door and entered the office the chief exclaimed, "Well now, here's a fine young man. This isn't your fault at all—it's your mother's fault for having such a handsome young son!'"

The chief was a young man with a slightly swarthy complexion and the educated air of one who'd been to university. His sudden exclamation made me feel wretched. I felt hideously disfigured, as if my face were half-covered with port wine stains.

He had the build of someone who practiced judo or kendo and, in stark contrast to the assiduous, lascivious questioning of the old policeman the night before, his interrogation was straightforward and to the point. When he'd finished and was putting the forms together to be sent to the prosecutor's office, he turned to me and said, "You really have to start taking better care of yourself. Look, you're coughing up blood, aren't you?"

I did have an odd cough that morning, and each time I coughed I would cover my mouth with my handkerchief. The handkerchief, spotted all over with blood, looked like it'd been pelted with red hail. But the blood wasn't from my coughing; it was from a boil on my ear that I'd been picking at the night before. It occurred to me then that things might go easier for me if I failed to correct the chief, so, eyes downcast and voice penitent, I simply said, "Yes," and left it at that.

The chief finished with the forms.

"It's all up to the prosecutor now. He'll decide whether or not to indict, but, in any event, you'd do well to call someone or send a telegram. Ask them to meet you at the Yokohama Prosecutor's Office so you can be released into their custody. Is there someone you can call? A guardian or someone who can vouch for you?"

I thought of Mr. Shibuta, my guarantor at school. He was

a short, fat man, a bachelor of about forty who came from the same village as me. He traded in art and antiques and was forever going in and out of Father's villa in Tokyo, playing the role of professional sycophant. His face, and his eyes in particular, had the look of a flounder, and that had become Father's nickname for him. I'd since picked up the habit as well.

I borrowed the policeman's phone book and, finding Flounder's number, called him and asked him to come down to the prosecutor's office. He spoke with an arrogance that was new for him but agreed to do as I asked in the end.

"Hey, you'd better sterilize that phone! He's coughing up blood, you know."

I heard the chief's voice boom all the way back in my holding cell.

Later that afternoon they tied a thin, hemp rope about my waist. I was allowed to cover it with my cloak but, even so, a young policeman gripped the other end of the rope tightly as we boarded the train to Yokohama.

I wasn't the slightest bit worried. I even felt a little nostalgic for my holding cell and for the old policeman, too. Why am I this way? Here I am, a criminal, all bound up, and this is when I feel calm and relaxed. Even now, writing these words, an easy happiness grows inside me.

Yet, even among these fond recollections, there was one misstep. One mistake so mortifying that I broke out in a cold sweat, a blunder I will never forget so long as I live. I was brought to the prosecutor's office—a dim, gloomy place—and underwent another, cursory interrogation. The prosecutor was a quiet man of about forty (if "beauty" had ever been ascribed to me, it was,

I do not doubt, nothing more than a base, lascivious beauty. The prosecutor, however, had what can only be called a "virtuous beauty," with its own aura of wisdom and tranquility). He didn't seem the type to be bothered by trifles, and I let my guard down entirely. I was answering his questions with a distracted air when I had another fit of coughing. I pulled my handkerchief from my sleeve and, thinking that I might as well make use of the opportunity, devised a despicable scheme. I added two more exaggerated, wheezing coughs, glancing out of the corner of my eye as I pressed the handkerchief to my mouth.

"Really?"

It was a gentle smile. I broke out in a cold sweat. I was horrified. No, even now the mere memory of it makes me want to jump to my feet. It is no exaggeration to say I felt even worse than I did in middle school student when that idiot, Takeichi, poking me in the back and calling me a "show off," sent me plummeting to the depths of hell. These were the two greatest blunders in my life of acting. So mortified was I that I sometimes think I'd rather have been sentenced to ten years in prison than be subjected to the prosecutor's gentle scorn.

In the end, I was given a suspended indictment. This didn't make me feel the slightest bit better. I sat on the bench outside the prosecutor's office, waiting for Flounder to fetch me, more miserable than I would've thought possible.

I stared out at the glow of the setting sun through the tall window. A line of seagulls seemed to form the Chinese character for "woman" as they flew past.

THE**THIRD**JOURNAL

Part One

One of Takeichi's predictions came true, the other did not. The one empty of honor, that women would fall for me, came true, while the more felicitous prediction that I would become a famous artist was never realized.

At best, I managed to become a third-rate, nameless cartoonist, publishing in lowbrow magazines.

I was expelled from school as a result of the Kamakura incident and spent my days in a tiny three-mat room on the second floor of Flounder's house. Each month a meager allowance arrived from home, but even that didn't reach my hands directly as it was sent in secret to Flounder (my brothers, it seemed, were sending it without my father's knowledge). All other ties with my family had been completely severed. Though I did my best to ingratiate myself with Flounder, he was forever in a bad mood and never even smiled at me. That people should prove so fickle and change so utterly at the drop of a hat seemed to me more comical than despicable.

"Stay inside. Just stay in your room." That's all he ever said to me.

I suppose he was afraid I would commit suicide. Believing I

might try to follow the woman into death and throw myself into the sea, he forbade me from going outside. In truth, he needn't have worried. Confined to my tiny room, spending my days and nights curled up under a blanket and reading old magazines like a halfwit, unable to drink or smoke, I'd completely lost the energy to kill myself.

Flounder's house was near the medical school in Okubo, not far from Hongō. Though his enthusiastically lettered sign boldly announced the presence of a purveyor of fine arts and antiques, the "Garden of the Green Dragon," his business was in fact nothing but one of two shops in a tiny row house, with a cramped doorway and, inside, shelves lined with useless rubbish, all covered in a thick layer of dust. (Flounder did not rely on the rubbish in his shop to support himself but rather earned his crust as a go-between—facilitating the transfer of one gentleman's treasures to another.) Flounder was hardly ever in the shop. He left early each morning with a scowl on his face, and, while he was gone, a shop boy of about seventeen or eighteen was responsible for keeping an eye on me. He spent every spare moment playing catch in the street with the other boys from the neighborhood. I was just a loafer on the second floor, an idiot or a madman, and he subjected me to any number of pompous lectures. Being averse to conflict, I meekly endured his pronouncements with an attitude that alternated between interest and exhaustion. It seemed he was Shibuta's—Flounder's—illegitimate son, but the situation was complicated and the connection not openly acknowledged. That Shibuta had never married may have been due in part to these complications. I seemed to recall hearing gossip to that effect when I was living at home but the affairs of others didn't hold much interest for me, so I don't know any of the details. Still, the set of the boy's eyes did have something of the look of a fish about them, so perhaps he really was Flounder's son. . . . If so, theirs was a cold and lonely relationship. Sometimes, they ordered soba noodles late at night and—without inviting me—ate in wordless silence.

It was the boy's job to prepare the meals, so, three times a day every day, he climbed the steps to the second floor, carrying a tray specially prepared for the pest who lived upstairs. He and Flounder would eat in the damp four-and-a-half mat room downstairs, and I could hear the clattering of dishes as they rushed through their meals.

One evening, toward the end of March, Flounder, who must have come into unexpected funds or perhaps had some other scheme in mind (it may have been a combination of the two, or any number of other possibilities that hadn't occurred to me), called me down from my room on the second floor and bade me join him at his table upon which, most unusually, there was tuna—not flounder—sashimi, and a bottle of warm saké. The master of the table, full of admiration at the luxury of his own banquet, absently offered me a dribble of saké.

"So, what exactly are you going to do with yourself?"

I didn't say anything but rather picked at a dish of dried sardines. I felt the warmth of mild intoxication wash over me as I gazed into the silver eyes of the dried fish. I longed for a return to the days when I caroused about town and even felt a certain nostalgia for Horiki. A desire for "freedom" began to build inside me, and at any moment I felt that tears would start trickling down my face.

Since arriving at Flounder's house I'd lost even the energy to play the clown and meekly surrendered myself to the scorn of Flounder and his boy. For his part, Flounder seemed keen to avoid long, frank talks with me, and I felt no desire to go chasing after him to plead my case. My transformation into a half-witted, freeloading houseguest was all but complete.

"Now look, this suspended indictment thing—it seems it won't leave any kind of record. Well then, you've got a chance to make a fresh start, if you make the effort. If you mend your ways and confide in me—I mean really confide in me—I'll give it some thought too."

Flounder—but no, not just Flounder but everyone, or so it seemed to me—spoke with a vague, wary edge to his words and with an odd complexity, perhaps due to the liberal sprinkling of verbal loopholes. It seemed a pointless, excessive caution. His endless, petty, annoying rhetorical acrobatics never failed to confound me and I soon gave up trying to follow him, either using my clowning to treat it like a joke or just sitting there, nodding my head in a silent attitude of utter defeat and letting him have his way entirely.

I didn't realize it until many years later, but had Flounder only outlined the situation as it really was everything could've been resolved without a fuss. His unnecessary caution or, rather, the incomprehensible pretension and posing that is all too common in this world, brought about indescribable misery.

All he had to do was say the following:

"We don't care if it's a national school or a private school but, come April, make sure that you are going to school. Do this and your family will take care of the expenses."

As I discovered much later, that is precisely how things stood. Had I known, I certainly would've done as I was told. It was Flounder's wary, roundabout manner of speaking that made everything sound strangely complicated, and, as a result, the direction of my life changed completely.

"Of course, if you have no intention of confiding in me then there is very little that I can do."

"Confide in you . . . about what?" I truly had no idea what he was getting at.

"About what's in your heart, surely."

"Such as?"

"Such as? Such as what you are going to do with yourself."

"You mean . . . You think I should get a job?"

"No, tell me what *you* think."

"But even if I wanted to go back to school . . ."

"Then you'd need money, of course. But the real problem isn't money. It's your feelings."

Why didn't he just tell me that the money would be sent from home? That would've settled my mind entirely, but instead I stumbled about aimlessly, lost in a fog with no idea which way to go.

"Well, how about it? Don't you have any goals? Any dreams for the future? I don't suppose the person being looked after has any idea how much trouble it is to take care of someone else all the time."

"I'm sorry."

"I'm really worried about you. Now that I've gone and taken on the job of looking after you I don't like to see this kind of apathy. I want you to show me you're determined to make a new start for yourself. A grand start. Now, if you come to me and, in all sincerity, confide your goals and plans for the future in me—why, I'll do everything I can to help. Now, it's only poor old Flounder here, so if you have any notions of returning to your old life of luxury you'd better give them up. But if you're determined, if you've set a clear course for the future, and if you confide in me then I have every intention of doing what I can to help, meager though that help might be. Do you see what I'm trying to say? Do you understand? What, precisely, do you, plan to do with yourself?"

"Well, if I can't stay here I'll get a job and . . ."

"Honestly? Is that what you're really thinking? These days even people from imperial universities . . ."

"Oh, no—I didn't mean a job at a company."

"What, then?"

"As an artist." I said with sudden resolve.

"Whaa-?"

I will never forget how Flounder looked at that moment, neck scrunched up as he laughed, a sly shadow across his face. Scornful yet also not. If I were to liken it to the sea, I suppose it would be akin to that strange, fluttering shadow that hovers over the deepest waters. In his laughter, I thought I had caught a flashing glimpse of the essence of adult life.

No, no, no, that simply won't do, you're not showing the slightest determination, think it over, take the night, think it over carefully. Thus instructed I hurried back upstairs, as though chased. I lay awake in bed but nothing came to me. So, sometime around dawn, I ran away.

I'll definitely be back by tonight. I'm going to discuss my

future with a friend at the address below. No need to worry. Honest.

With pencil and stationery, I scribbled the note in large letters and, adding Horiki's address, snuck out of Flounder's house.

I wasn't running away because I felt humiliated by Flounder's lecture. I ran away because I was of his mind entirely. I *did* lack determination. I had absolutely no idea what I should do with myself and, what is more, I genuinely felt sorry for Flounder. I was a constant irritation to him and a burden to his household. Even if, by some miracle, I should manage to rouse myself and resolve on a new course of action, when I thought of Flounder, poor as he was, sending me money each month, it pained me so much that I couldn't possibly stay any longer.

I wasn't really intending to discuss my so-called "plans for the future" with the likes of Horiki. I only wrote that to put Flounder's mind at ease, even if only for a little while (not in the hope of "throwing him off my scent" like you'd see in a detective novel—well no, I'm sure that must have been a consideration, though only a very slight one—rather, better to say I was terrified that Flounder, shocked by my sudden disappearance, would grow confused, violently agitated. It was a typical, pathetic tendency of mine. I know from the start I'll be found out but I'm too timid to tell the truth so I always dress it up. I'm not unlike those creatures that society reviles as "liars," but I hardly ever seek to conceal the truth out of a desire for personal gain. I almost always act out of desperation, on the spur of the moment, when a sudden chill descends on a room and I feel like I'm suffocating. I know I will pay for it later but when my desperate "need to please" rears its head I'm suddenly adding some strange, feeble,

idiotic embellishment or other. I've been much criticized for this
by the so-called "honest people" of the world), and Horiki's name
just popped into my head so I scribbled it in the margins—there
was nothing more to it than that.

I walked a little ways to Shinjuku and sold the books I'd
taken with me. That done, as you might suppose, I had absolutely no idea what to do next. I got along with almost everyone,
but I'd never known true "friendship." Drinking friends like
Horiki aside, all my interactions with other people were nothing more than exercises in suffering. I played the clown in the
hopes of mitigating that suffering, but the clowning itself left me
exhausted. If I saw someone on the street with whom I had even
the slightest acquaintance, or even someone who looked like an
acquaintance, I gave a sudden start; a shudder of disgust rippled
through me, leaving me dizzy. I was well liked by others, but it
seems I lacked the ability to love them back. (Or rather, let's say
I have grave doubts as to whether or not anyone in this world
possesses the ability to "love.") It was only natural, then, that a
person like me would not have any "close friends." It was all but
impossible for me to even "visit" people. The gates of another's
house were more disturbing to me than the gates of hell in *The
Divine Comedy*. Somewhere, I knew, in those depths beyond the
gate, a terrible beast lurked, a dragon writhed, filling the air with
the stench of rotting meat.

I had no friends. I had no place to go.

Horiki.

I'd meant it as a joke but in the end I did just as I wrote in my
letter. I went to see Horiki in Asakusa. This was the first time I'd
actually gone to see him at home. Before I'd just sent telegrams,

telling him to come and meet me, but now I begrudged even the telegram fee and, disgraced as I was, I wasn't certain that a telegram would be sufficient to bring him out. So I resigned myself to doing what I disliked most and decided to pay Horiki a visit. With a heavy sigh I climbed aboard a streetcar, and, when it occurred to me that the sole ray of hope left to me in this world was none other than Horiki, a terrible wave of foreboding swept over me, sending shivers down my spine.

He was at home. His was a tiny two-story house at the end of a filthy alleyway. He lived in a six-mat room that occupied the entirety of the second floor while his aged parents and a young craftsman sewed and pounded away on the first floor, making thongs for *geta* sandals.

On that day Horiki showed me a new aspect of his "city boy" persona. It was his cunning. A display of such cold, calculated egotism as to leave a simple country boy like me utterly astounded. He was not, it seemed, someone who simply drifted aimlessly through life as I did.

"You're hopeless! Has your father forgiven you yet? No?"

I couldn't tell him that I'd run away.

As was my wont, I lied. Though I knew Horiki would discover the truth at any moment, I lied.

"Oh, it'll work out one way or another."

"Hey, this is no joke. I'm warning you—you'd better wise up. Even an idiot knows when enough is enough. Look, I've got things to do—I'm really busy these days."

"Things? What kind of things?"

"Hey! Stop that! Don't pick at the cushion!"

I'd been unconsciously fingering the threads at the seam or

hem or whatever it's called—that bundle of threads on the corner of the cushion—and yanking on them. When it came to his own possessions Horiki despised the loss of a single thread. Far from being embarrassed at his own outburst, he glared at me in rebuke. I suddenly realized that, over the course of our association, Horiki had not lost so much as a single thing.

His mother came up the stairs, carrying a tray with two bowls of sweet adzuki bean soup and rice cakes.

"Oh, thank you!" Horiki spoke with such unnatural politeness and reserve that one could almost believe him to be a true, filial son.

"Thank you so much—adzuki and rice cake, is it? Oh, that's too much! You really shouldn't have put yourself to so much trouble. I have to go out soon. No, no—please leave it. After all, it is your famous adzuki soup and it would be a shame to waste it. Thank you. Here, you have some too—Mother made it especially for us. Ah, now this is excellent. Wonderful!"

He was so delighted and ate with such relish that I couldn't think it entirely an act. I sipped at the soup, but it smelled of boiled water and, when I took a bite of the rice cake, I realized it wasn't rice cake at all but something I couldn't identify. I am certainly not scorning their poverty. (Indeed, at the time I thought the soup wasn't bad, and I was touched by his mother's consideration. Though I lived in terror of poverty, I don't think that I scorned it in others.) The soup, and Horiki's obvious delight in it, showed me the frugal character of the urbanite as well as the true nature of the Tokyo family, with its clear distinction between insider and outsider. I describe this scene simply to record the profound feeling of loneliness and confusion that swept over me as I sat there, plying my chipped and worn chopsticks. I alone had been left behind, a fool, forever fleeing from human society, with no regard for the distinctions of insider and outsider, abandoned even by Horiki.

"Sorry, but I've got things to do," Horiki said, standing up and putting on his jacket. "Got to go. Sorry."

At that moment a female visitor arrived for Horiki, and the direction of my life changed completely.

Horiki brightened suddenly. "Oh, I'm sorry—I was just about to go and pay a visit on you but then this one here showed up. No, no, not at all—please come in. Have a seat."

Horiki seemed very agitated. I'd gotten up from the cushion I'd been sitting on and, turning it over, held it out for the visitor, but Horiki, snatching it from me, turned it over again before offering it to the woman. There were only the two cushions in the room, Horiki's and the one for guests.

The woman was tall and thin. She sat politely beside the cushion, in the corner of the room by the doorway.

I listened absently to their conversation. She apparently worked for a magazine that had commissioned a print or the like from Horiki and she'd come to pick it up.

"We are in rather a hurry."

"It's done—I finished it ages ago. Here you are."

A telegram arrived.

Horiki's good humor faded as he read, his smile replaced by a scowl.

"Dammit—what've you done now?"

The telegram was from Flounder.

"Anyway, just go home. I ought to take you there myself but

I'm too busy for that now. What were you thinking, sitting there looking so pleased with yourself when you've just run away from home!"

"Where do you live?"

"In Okubo," I replied without thinking.

"Well, that's not far from my office."

She was twenty-eight, from Kōshū, amid the mountains. She lived in an apartment out in Kōenji with her five-year-old daughter. It had been three years since her husband died, she said.

"You look like you went through a lot growing up. You're so sensitive, poor thing."

That was my first time living as a kept man. When Shizuko (for that was her name) left for work at the magazine in Shinjuku I stayed home, dutifully caring for her daughter, Shigeko. Before I came along she'd play at the superintendent's apartment while her mother worked, but now she seemed wholly taken with this new, "sensitive" man who'd shown up to be her playmate.

I'd been there for a week or so, idly whiling the time away. Power lines ran near the window and a kite decorated with a colorful drawing of an old-fashioned houseboy had become entangled in them, tossing this way and that, torn in places by the strong, dusty spring winds. Still, it clung tenaciously to the wire, bouncing back and forth as though bobbing its head in agreement. I grimaced and reddened each time I saw it. It even appeared in my dreams, making me groan in my sleep.

"I want . . . some money."

"How much?"

"A lot. . . . It's true what they say, you know. When poverty comes in, love flies out."

"Don't be silly. That's just old-fashioned nonsense. . . ."

"Is it, though? How can you tell? If things stay like this I might run off one of these days."

"Which of us is poor? And which of us is going to run off? You're being silly."

"I want to earn my own money to buy liquor—no, cigarettes. I think my paintings are a lot better than Horiki's."

At times like this, memories of the self-portraits I'd painted in middle school—what Takeichi called my "monster paintings"—rose up, unbidden, from the depths of my mind. My lost masterpieces. They'd vanished over the many times I'd moved, but I couldn't help thinking that they in particular had been truly superb. I had painted any number of pictures since, but those remembered masterpieces seemed now so impossibly distant I was left feeling hollow and plagued by the dull ache of loss.

A half-empty glass of absinthe.

That is how I secretly described that eternal, irreparable sense of loss. Whenever people talked about paintings, that half-empty glass of absinthe flitted before my eyes and I grew restless. I writhed with the desire to show them my lost paintings, to convince them of my talent.

She snickered. "Really? It's so cute the way you joke with a straight face."

I'm not joking! It's true! Oh, I wish I could show you. After a moment's idle anguish, however, I gave up and changed tack. "Cartoons, then. At least I can outdo Horiki when it comes to cartoons."

I was ignored when I was serious, and only when I was

clowning and deceiving, as now, did my words seem to carry a ring of truth.

"That's not a bad idea. I was impressed, to be honest. I've seen the ones you're always drawing for Shigeko and they even make me laugh. How about it? Want to give it a try? I can talk to the editor at work."

Her company published an obscure monthly magazine for children.

When women see you ... We can't help ourselves. We feel compelled to do something, to help. . . . You're always so timid and yet still a comedian. . . . Sometimes, you get so lonely and depressed but when women see this, we only want to help you all the more.

Shizuko often said things like that, flattering and coaxing me. Yet, when it occurred to me that her remarks possessed the unwholesome quality specific to words addressed to a kept man they had the opposite effect and I found myself sinking even further, unable to rouse even a glimmer of spirit. I wanted money, not women. I secretly yearned and schemed for some means to support myself, enabling me to escape from Shizuko, but, in the end, these schemes only made me more reliant upon her. She took care of the mess I left behind when I ran away just as she took care of everything else. This woman from Kōshū was more formidable than any man, and it wasn't long before I had to "tremble" before Shizuko too.

She set up a meeting between herself, Flounder, and Horiki where it was decided that all remaining ties with my family would be severed and Shizuko and I would live openly as husband and wife. Furthermore, thanks to Shizuko's deft maneuverings, my cartoons were bringing in surprisingly large amounts of money.

Even as I spent that money on liquor and cigarettes, my feelings of loneliness and gloom only grew worse with each passing day. I'd sunk so low that there were times when, drawing "The Adventures of Kinta and Ota" for Shizuko's magazine, I would suddenly find myself so overwhelmed by longing for my family back home that my pen ceased its scratching and, my head hanging, tears began to spill from my eyes.

At such times Shigeko was my faint salvation. She'd already taken to calling me "Daddy" without the slightest self-consciousness.

"Daddy, is it true? If you pray to God he'll give you whatever you want?"

If so, I'm the one who should be praying, I thought.

Oh Lord, grant me cold determination. Grant me understanding of the nature of "humans." It is no sin even to shove another aside. Oh God, grant me the mask of anger.

"Yes, that's right. God will give you anything you ask for, but I don't think it'll work for me."

I was terrified even of God. I couldn't bring myself to trust in God's love, I could only believe in His wrath. Faith. To me, that meant standing before the judgment seat, head hung low, waiting to be scourged by His whip. I could believe in hell readily enough but the idea of heaven was beyond me.

"Why not?"

"Because I didn't obey my parents."

"Really? But everyone says you're good."

That's because I'm deceiving them. I knew as well as she did that everyone in the building was fond of me. But I was terrified of them all, and the more terrified I was the more they liked me.

The more they liked me, the more terrified I became. I wanted to escape from all of them. But it was far too difficult to explain this unfortunate malady of mine to Shigeko.

"What will you ask God for?" I asked, casually changing the topic.

"I, I want my real daddy."

I felt like I'd been punched in the stomach, my vision swam. An enemy. I don't know if I was Shigeko's enemy or if she was mine, but in the end here too was yet another terrifying adult, threatening me. A stranger, an incomprehensible stranger, a stranger full of secrets. That is how Shigeko appeared to me then.

At least I have Shigeko, or so I had thought. Yet, in the end this one too had a tail that could "crush the life from a horsefly with a single blow." From that point on I trembled before even her.

"Hey, pervert! You there?"

Horiki started visiting again. He'd caused me such profound sadness the day I ran away, but still I couldn't refuse him, and I greeted him with a weak smile.

"So, looks like your cartoons are quite the thing. That's the world for you, I guess—fools rush in where angels fear to tread. Must be true. Don't let it go to your head, though—your sketching is still a joke."

Who did he think he was, putting on airs as though he were a master? How would he react if I showed him one of my monster paintings? Even as I lapsed into my usual, idle writhing I replied, "Now, don't say such things. You'll only make me scream."

He seemed to grow smugger still.

"Well, when your only talent is for getting ahead in the world people will see through you eventually."

A talent for getting ahead in the world? Honestly, I could only grimace in reply. Me? A talent for getting ahead in the world! Yet, perhaps there was something to what he said. Perhaps people like me, those who live in terror of human beings, who seek to avoid them at any cost, who deceive them—perhaps, in some strange way, these things worked in our favor. Perhaps we look like people who conscientiously observed that cunning old saying, "let sleeping dogs lie." Oh, people don't know the first thing about one another. They think themselves the very best of friends even as they utterly fail to understand each other. They live their whole lives thus, never realizing their mistake, and when one of them dies, they weep as they give the eulogy.

Horiki (reluctantly, I'm sure, and only at Shizuko's prodding) helped clean up the mess after I ran away from Flounder's, so, perhaps because of this, he had convinced himself that my new start in life was all thanks to him. As though he were the one who had united me with Shizuko. So, he solemnly subjected me to lectures, showed up drunk in the middle of the night searching for a place to sleep, or came over to borrow five yen (always five yen).

"Well, I hope you've put your womanizing days behind you now. Society won't tolerate any more of it, you know."

What exactly was society? A plurality of people? Where, precisely, was the material form of this thing called society located? I'd lived my whole life in terror of society, imagining it to be something strong, forbidding, frightening. Yet, as Horiki spoke, it suddenly came to me.

"When you say society, you mean you, right?"

The words rose to the tip of my tongue but I swallowed them, not wanting to anger Horiki.

(Society won't tolerate it.)

(It's not society. It's you who won't tolerate it, right?)

(If you go on doing things like that, society won't go easy on you.)

(It's not society, though, is it? It's you.)

(Society will bury you alive.)

(It's not society. It's you who will bury me, isn't it?)

Know thyself. Know thy terrifying, strange, wily, villainous, crone-like self!

Such thoughts flitted across my mind, but, in the end, I merely wiped the sweat from my brow with my handkerchief and, laughing, said, "You've got me in a cold sweat!"

Ever since this encounter I've maintained this quasi-philosophical belief (is not society nothing more than the individual?).

And, having arrived at the realization that society is nothing more than the individual, it became much easier for me to act in accord with my own wishes. Or, in Shizuko's words, I became a little more selfish and less timid. Or, in Horiki's words, I grew stingy. Or, in Shigeko's words, I didn't play with her as much.

I passed each day in grim silence, looking after Shigeko, filling orders for cartoons (I occasionally received orders from other publishers too but they were all third-rate magazines, even cruder than Shizuko's). I drew "The Adventures of Kinta and Ota" or "The Happy-Go-Lucky Priest"—a brazen copy of "The Happy-Go-Lucky Dad"—or other, silly cartoons such as "Hasty Pin-chan," which even I didn't understand. Deep in my melancholy I drew sluggishly (I draw very slowly), my only thought being to earn money for drinking. The moment Shizuko got back from work I rushed out the door, as though it were the changing of shifts, and headed straight for the cheap standing bars near Kōenji Station where I drank cheap, strong liquor until I began to feel a bit more cheerful. Then, going home,

"You know . . . The more I look at you the stranger you look. Did you know your face was the inspiration for the Happy-Go-Lucky Priest? I got the idea watching you sleep."

"Well, you look really old when you sleep. Like you're in your forties."

"It's your fault. You suck the life right out of me. Like the rushing of waters, so go lives of men." I sang, "Why do you fret so? As the willow on the banks of the streeeam."

"Stop making such a racket and go to bed. Or would you like something to eat?" She was always so calm, as though she wasn't paying any attention to me at all.

"I'll have a drink if we have anything. Like the rushing of water, so go lives of men. Like the rushing of men . . . no, water, so goes the life of water."

Shizuko undressed me as I sang and, head pressed to Shizuko's breast, I fell asleep. Such was my routine.

> And thus we begin again the next day,
> Under the same, settled rules of the past
> If only we might avoid great, violent joys
> So too will we escape great sorrows.
> As the toad hops around
> The stone blocking his path.

When I first read this translation—originally from a poem by Guy Charles Cros, I think—I flushed a crimson so deep my face seemed to burn.

A toad.

(That's all I am. It makes no difference if society forgives me or not, if it buries me or not. I am lower even than a dog or a cat. A toad. Just plodding along.)

I began to drink more and more. I no longer confined myself to the bars around Kōenji Station but ventured out to Shinjuku and Ginza, sometimes not coming home until the following day. All I wanted was to avoid the "settled rules of the past." I played the scoundrel in bars, kissing every girl I saw, reverting to the same wild drunk I'd been before the love suicide. No, I was worse. I even started selling off Shizuko's clothes when I ran out of money.

One night, over a year after I found myself grimacing at the tangled kite outside the window, just after the cherry blossoms had scattered, I smuggled some of Shizuko's underrobes and *obi* out of the house and pawned them. With money in my pocket, I went drinking in Ginza and stayed out for two nights running. But by the third night, even I couldn't help feeling a little bad, and I went back home. Walking with unconscious stealth, I went up to the door to Shizuko's room. Shigeko and Shizuko were inside, talking.

"Why does he drink?"

"Daddy doesn't drink because he likes it. It's just that he's too good so, so . . ."

"Do all good people drink?"

"Well, no, it's not that but . . ."

"I bet Daddy'll be surprised, won't he?"

"He might not be very happy. Look, now, he's jumped out of the box."

"He's just like Hasty Pin-chan, isn't he?"

"Yes, he is." Shizuko said with a soft, contented laugh.

I slid the door open a crack and peeked inside. A tiny white rabbit jumped here and there as mother and daughter chased after it.

(They are happy. These are happy people. And here I am, an idiot, blundering into their midst, destroying everything. Simple joy. A good mother and daughter. Oh Lord, if you listen to the prayers of people like me, just once, just once in my life, I beg you.)

I felt like dropping to my knees and clasping my hands in prayer right there. Silently, I slid the door shut, went back to Ginza, and never again returned to that apartment.

So it was that I came to take up residence on the second floor of a downtown standing bar in Kyōbashi, a kept man once again.

Society. I felt I was beginning to understand it, if only vaguely. It was a struggle between one individual and another, and it was a struggle that took place at a specific moment in time, and all you needed to do was to win in that moment. No one person can conquer another entirely, and even a slave can manage a slave's servile riposte, so all we can do is bet everything on a single throw of the dice, an all-or-nothing bet, right then and there. There's no other way to go through life. People sing the praises of honor and loyalty, but the sole focus of all human endeavor is the individual. Beyond the individual there is but another individual. The inscrutability of society, the sea is not society—it is the individual. In this way I was somewhat liberated from my terror of that mirage, that vast ocean of the world. I no longer felt compelled to display the same infinite consideration toward all matters, behaving instead with a degree of casual disregard for others as the situation and moment required.

I abandoned the apartment in Kōenji, went over to the Madam of the standing bar in Kyōbashi and said, "I've left her."

That was all I said and that was all that needed to be said. I had won the all-or-nothing bet, and, perhaps a bit too aggressively, had made a place for myself on the second floor of the bar. Yet, society—that "society" I was supposed to regard with such trepidation—did not inflict the slightest injury upon me. Nor did I attempt to defend or justify myself to "society." So long as the Madam was willing, that was all that mattered.

I was part customer, part owner, part errand boy, and part relative. To an outsider I suppose I must have seemed an odd creature indeed, but "society" didn't pay the slightest heed to me, and the regulars were all terribly kind, calling out, "Yō-chan, Yō-chan" and buying me drinks.

The sense of caution I had maintained toward the world gradually began to fade. It might not be such a terrifying place after all. The terror that had so consumed me before seemed now more like superstition. Like the "scientific myths" that the spring winds carry millions of whooping cough germs, or that the public baths teem with bacteria that make you go blind, the millions of germs in a barbershop that cause baldness, handle straps in trains contaminated with scabies, undercooked pork and beef, sashimi infested with tapeworm, flatworm and so on, that if you stepped barefoot on a tiny shard of glass it would find its way into your bloodstream and put out your eye. "Scientifically," I am sure there are millions of bacteria floating and swimming about wherever we go. I came to realize, however, that all we needed do was ignore these facts entirely and they lost their hold over us, vanishing entirely in the end, reduced to nothing more than "scientific ghosts." Just as when people go on about how if you throw away three grains of rice with your lunch and ten million other people do the same then so many bushels of rice are wasted, or when they say that if ten million people conserved just one tissue each day then so many tons of pulp would be saved, and so on. How terrified I used to be of this kind of "scientific accounting." Whenever I wasted so much as a single grain of rice, each time I blew my nose I was haunted by visions of a mountain of rice, of mountains of pulp going to waste. I grew despondent, as if I'd committed some terrible crime. Yet, in the end, these were but "scientific lies," "statistical lies," "mathematical lies." Nobody was going to go around and collect each of those three grains of rice. Even purely as an intellectual exercise in mathematics it was a silly, primitive notion—no better those idiotic statistics exercises where one calculates the probability of a person tripping in the dark and falling into the toilet or the number of passengers who would get a leg stuck in the gap between train and platform. They sound plausible enough, but I've never heard of anyone getting hurt by falling into the toilet. I was gradually learning to see the world for what it was, and I wanted to laugh at myself for having lived in such terror of these hypotheticals, of these "scientific facts" that had been drilled into me and which I had taken as real.

All that was true, but people still scared me and I had to fortify myself with a drink before meeting them, even customers in the bar. After all, I'd seen terrifying things. Yet I still went out to the bar each night, drank with them, and even argued absurd theories of art with them. I was like the child who, frightened of an animal, will run up to it and hug it all the tighter for all that.

A cartoonist. Ah, I was but an unknown cartoonist with neither great joy nor great sadness. I secretly ached for a great, violent joy and to hell with whatever sadness might follow, no matter how terrible it might be. But my only joys, if they can be called such, were getting embroiled in pointless debates with the customers and drinking their liquor.

This tedious life at Kyōbashi continued for nearly a year, and I was now selling my cartoons to other magazines too—not just children's magazines. I drew for the cheap, dirty magazines you find at station newsstands. I drew coarse nudes under the absurd pen name of "Jōshi Ikita" (a homophone for "survived love suicide"), appending a verse from *The Rubaiyat* to each.

> Why not abandon your futile prayers
> And cast off those worries that invite tears
> Come now, let's drink and talk of fond memories
> Forgetting a while our cares.

> People who menace with worry and terror,
> Trembling before their imagined sins
> Forever scheming and plotting
> Against the spirits' vengeance.

> Yester eve, stomach full of wine and heart full of joy
> The morn stirs, so bleak and desolate

How treacherous the night
To thus my feelings break.

Forget the damnation to come
That haunts us with dim fear
Like the echo of a distant drum
The tallying of petty sins behooves none.

Is it righteousness, then, that is man's compass?
Yet, what justice then lies
In the blood-soaked battlefield
Or on the tip of an assassin's knife?

Where have the guiding principles gone?
What profound wisdom now lights the way?
It is both beautiful and terrible, this floating world.
We but delicate children, forced to bear the unbearable.

Always the seed of desire is planted, yet with it we can
do naught.
Good, Bad, Sin, Punishment, so we are cursed.
Always wandering, helpless.
Never permitted the strength of will to crush it.

Where and why do you wander?
What do you censure, survey, remember?
Ha! It is but an empty dream, a feeble illusion
Aha! We forget our wine, all is idle musing.

Gaze up now at the boundless sky!
There, a tiny speck floating within.
As if we could know why the earth spins.
Spin, whirl, or roll over—it shall do as it likes.

Everywhere I go, I sense unrivaled power.
On every land, in every people,
I discover the same humanity.
Could it be that I am the heretic?

All misread the holy book
Else they lack wisdom and sense,
To forbid the wine, to forgo the pleasures of living
flesh,
Do as you will, Mustafa. Such things I detest.

It was around this time that a young girl urged me to stop
drinking.

"You can't go on like this. Drunk by noon every day."

Her name was Yoshiko, though I called her Yoshi-chan, and
she worked at a tiny tobacconist across the street from the bar.
About seventeen or eighteen, she was pale-skinned with slightly
crooked teeth. She smiled and offered the same warning each
time I went to buy cigarettes.

"Why not? What's wrong with it? As they said in ancient
Persia, 'Drink all the wine, dear child, and dispel hatred—Away!
Away!' Anyway, it doesn't matter. The jade chalice of oblivion, as
the poet says, is the only hope for this heart, heavy and worn with
sorrow. You see?"

"Nope."

"Why you—keep it up and I'll kiss you."

"Go on then," she said with a pout, not looking remotely abashed.

"You idiot. No notion of chastity . . ."

Yet from her expression, it was clear that she remained a virgin, untouched by any man.

On one particularly cold night after New Year's I got drunk and went to buy cigarettes when I fell into an open manhole right in front of the tobacconist. I cried out to Yoshi-chan for help, and she pulled me out and tended the cut on my right arm. "You drink too much," she said, unsmiling, her voice thick with emotion.

The thought of dying didn't bother me in the slightest, but when it came to injuries, bleeding and the like, I wanted none of it. As she cleaned the cut on my arm I started to think that perhaps I really had better stop drinking.

"I'll give it up. From tomorrow. I won't touch a drop of the stuff."

"Really?"

"Absolutely. I'll quit. And if I do you'll be my bride, right?"

I'd meant the bit about her being my bride as a joke.

"OC!"

"OC" was short for "of course." Like "mobo" for modern boy and "moga" for modern girl, abbreviating things was all the rage back then.

"All right, shake on it then. I'm definitely quitting."

Of course, I'd started drinking again by noon the next day.

That evening I stumbled outside and made my way over to Yoshi-chan's shop.

"Yoshi-chan, sorry! I got drunk again."

"What's this? That's not very nice, pretending to be drunk!"

I gasped. I even started to feel sober.

"But it's true. I'm not pretending—I really am drunk."

"You shouldn't tease me, it's not nice," she said, guilelessly.

"But all you have to do is look at me. I started drinking at noon today, too. Forgive me?"

"You put on a good act, don't you?"

"I'm not acting, you idiot! Keep it up and I'll kiss you!"

"Go on, then."

"No, I don't have the right to. I must abandon my plan of taking you as my bride. Look at me—my face is red, right? I'm drunk."

"That's just from the sunset. You can't fool me. You promised to stop drinking yesterday so you can't be drunk. We even shook on it. I don't believe you. You're lying. Lies, lies, lies!"

I stood there gazing at her pale, smiling face, glowing in the dim light of the shop. How precious, I thought. This unsullied virginity. I'd never slept with a virgin younger than myself before. We should marry. Let whatever sadness comes, come, I don't care how terrible it is. Just once in my life I want to feel a great, violent joy. I'd always thought that "beautiful virginity" was simply a sentimental conceit employed by feeble-minded poets, but now I could see that it really did exist. In that instant I decided we'd marry, and in the springtime we'd ride our bicycles to a waterfall deep in the forest. It was an all-or-nothing bet, so, without a moment's hesitation, I stretched out my hand and snatched the flower.

We married soon thereafter, and while the joy I gained was

modest, the sadness—no, even the word misery falls short of the mark— that came after was terrible beyond all imagining. "The world," it seems, really was an infinitely terrifying place after all. It is certainly not the amiable sort of place where everything is decided with a single throw of the dice.

Part Two

Horiki and myself.

To scorn one another, to reduce one another to mediocrity. If this is what is meant by "friendship" then Horiki and I were the epitome of "friends."

Thanks entirely to the chivalry of the Madam from Kyōbashi (it may sound odd to speak of chivalry in a woman but experience has taught me—at least in the city—that women possess the quality of what I can only call chivalry in far greater quantities than men. Men, as a rule, are cowardly, trembling creatures who care for nothing but appearances and are stingy to boot), I succeeded in making Yoshiko my common-law wife. We rented a small room in eastern Tokyo on the first floor of a tiny two-story apartment in Tsukiji, near the Sumida River. I quit drinking and dedicated myself to what was, it seemed, becoming my chosen path—cartoons. After dinner we went to the movies and on the way home stopped at a coffee shop or bought a flower pot and so on. More than anything, I loved to simply listen to her and to gaze at her, this woman who trusted me to the very core of her being. It was around then that I started to think that I might, just possibly, be turning into something that resembled a human being. I began to feel a faint, warm hope that I might avoid a miserable death after all, when Horiki reappeared at my doorstep.

"Hey pervert! Well, now—what's this? Could you be turning respectable? I come bearing tidings from the Lady of Kōenji," he began but suddenly dropped his voice. He gave a jerk of his chin in the direction of Yoshiko in the kitchen, as though to see if it was safe to talk.

"It's fine. You can say whatever you like," I replied calmly.

Indeed, I think Yoshiko had a divine gift for trusting people. She never suspected anything about my relationship with the Madam from Kyōbashi, and even when I told her about the Kamakura incident she didn't believe there had been anything between Tsuneko and me. Not because I was a particularly gifted liar. Sometimes I even made a point of speaking as frankly and candidly as I could, but she just dismissed everything as a joke.

"Well, I can see you're doing well for yourself—same as always. In any case, it's nothing important. She just wanted me to tell you to come and visit her sometime."

Just as I am on the verge of forgetting, that winged monster dives, its beak ripping open the scab of memory. Vivid images of past sins and past shames suddenly unfold before my eyes and I grow so terrified that I want to scream. I can't sit still.

> Me: "Go for a drink?"
> Horiki: "Sure."

Me and Horiki. Cast from the same mold. We are, I sometimes thought, all but indistinguishable from one another. This only held true when we were together drinking cheap liquor;

when we went out we transformed into the same dog with the same coat of fur, sniffing around the snowy alleys of the red-light district.

From that day we rekindled our old friendship, we'd go back to the tiny Kyōbashi bar, too and, in the end, we two drunken dogs would find our way back to Shizuko's apartment in Kōenji, sometimes even spending the night there before heading home in the morning.

I will never forget. It was a hot, muggy summer evening. Sometime around sunset Horiki showed up at our apartment wearing a threadbare *yukata*. Due to "various circumstances" he'd pawned his summer clothes, but there would be trouble if his mother found out so he needed to redeem them as soon as possible and would I lend him the money? Unfortunately, we didn't have any money either, so, as was my usual practice, I sent Yoshiko off to pawn some of her clothes and, as the sum she received was slightly more than what Horiki required, I had her buy some *shōchū* liquor with the rest and we went up to the roof where we bathed in the feeble, muddy breeze that occasionally wafted in from the Sumida River and held a thoroughly squalid summer banquet.

We played a game of my own invention that consisted of categorizing nouns as either "comic" or "tragic." Just as nouns were divided into masculine, feminine, neutral, and so on, I thought it only proper that they should also be divided into the comic and the tragic. For example, steamer and steam locomotive are both tragic nouns whereas bus and streetcar are comic. Why? If you have to ask then clearly you are not qualified to discuss such weighty matters of art. Just as a playwright who allowed so much as a single tragic noun to find its way into a comedy would be scorned, so too would a tragedy that contained a comic noun.

"Ready? How about tobacco?" I asked.

"Trag (our abbreviation for tragedy)," Horiki said almost before I finished.

"Medicine?"

"Powder or pills?"

"Injections."

"Trag."

"Really? It might just be a hormone injection."

"No, trag. Absolutely trag. Come on, it's the needles—could anything be more trag?"

"All right, you win. But, you know, medicine and doctors—they're actually com (our abbreviation for comedy). What about death?"

"Com. Pastors and Buddhist priests, too."

"Bravo. So, I suppose that life is trag."

"No, that's com too."

"No, if we do that then everything will be com. All right, I'll try one more, then. Cartoonist. Surely *that* can't be com."

"Tragedy, tragedy. An epic tragedy."

"What's that? Surely *you're* the epic tragedy."

There was nothing remarkable about our feeble wordplay but, at the time, it seemed to us a most refined amusement, the likes of which had never graced the finest salons of the world—and we were absurdly proud of it.

Around the same time I'd invented another, similar game where the players had to guess the antonyms for words. The ant (an abbreviation for antonym) for black was white. However, the ant for white was red and the ant for red, black.

"What's the ant for flower?" I asked.

Horiki frowned slightly as he considered. "Well, there's a restaurant called 'Moon and Flowers' so it must be moon."

"No, no. That's not an ant. If it's anything, it's a synonym. Among the poets even stars and violets are synonyms, right? Not ants."

"OK, OK. Then, let's see . . . bees!"

"Bees?"

"'Atop the peonies . . . ' as the poem goes. . . . Or was it an ant?"

"Come now, that's a motif—you can't fool me."

"I've got it! 'Gathering clouds obscure the flowers . . . '"

"It's supposed to be 'Gathering clouds obscure the moon.'"

"Oh yeah, that's right. A wind scatters the flowers. It's the wind. The ant of flowers is the wind."

"I don't like it. It sounds like something you'd get from a wandering minstrel. Your true colors are starting to show."

"No, I've got it—it's the loquat. Same shape as your minstrel's lute."

"That's even worse. The ant for flowers . . . What is the one thing in the world that is most unlike flowers? That's what you need to find . . ."

"In that case . . . hang on. I've got it! It's 'woman.'"

"And while you're at it, the synonym for woman is?"

"Tripe."

"You, it seems, are wholly ignorant of the art of poesy. Give us the ant for tripe, then."

"Milk."

"That's not half bad. One more in that vein, then: shame. What's the ant?"

"Shameless. The famous cartoonist, Jōshi Ikita."

"What about Horiki Masao?"

Our laughter gradually began to fade as we succumbed to that mood particular to *shōchū*, that gloomy drunkenness, where your head feels like it is filled with shards of broken glass.

"Don't be a smart aleck. At least I've never been marched across the city with a rope tied about my waist."

I froze. It suddenly dawned on me that, all this time, Horiki had never really seen me as having turned over a new leaf. To him I was still nothing more than a shameless, stupid ghost who had even managed to fail at dying, a "living corpse." When he could use me for his own amusement, he did so. That was the extent of our "friendship." As you might expect, this realization did nothing to cheer me but, given the circumstances, it was only natural that Horiki should feel this way. Ever since I was a child I'd failed at being human so it was only right that I be scorned, even by the likes of Horiki.

"Crime. What's the antonym for crime, I wonder? This is a tough one," I said, feigning bland indifference.

"Law, of course." His response was so blasé that I looked up, considering him. The flickering red glow of the neon light from a nearby building gave his expression a particularly grim look, and the flinty, pitiless features of a detective. I was utterly taken aback.

"That's not what crime is, you know. Not at all."

Law? The antonym of crime! Yet, perhaps that kind of

simplistic thinking is typical of people in society. The belief that crime flourishes when there are no detectives around.

"Well what, then? God? You do have the stink of a Christian priest about you, after all. A bit disgusting, really."

"Now let's not be so hasty. We should put our heads together for this one. It's an interesting problem, no? I suspect we might learn all there is to know about a man by the way he answers this question."

"Don't be ridiculous. The ant for crime is . . . virtue. A virtuous citizen. That is to say, someone like me."

"Enough joking. Anyway, virtue is the ant for evil. It's not the ant for crime."

"So crime and evil are different, then?"

"Yes. I think so. Virtue and evil are human concepts. They're moral terms arbitrarily made up by human beings."

"You never shut up, do you? All right, then, it must be God after all. God, God, God. You can't go wrong by putting everything on God. Damn, I'm hungry."

"Yoshiko's boiling some broad beans for us now."

"Excellent. Love 'em."

He lay back, arms crossed behind his head.

"It's almost as though you don't care about crime at all."

"Of course not. I'm not a criminal like you, after all. I like to have a good time and all but I don't go around getting women killed or stealing their money."

Deep in my heart an echo, faint and desperate, welled up in protest. I didn't kill her. I didn't steal anyone's money. As usual, however, my resolve soon wavered. It was my fault, after all.

I was incapable of a straightforward argument. The gloom

brought on by the *shōchū* made me more irascible by the minute, and it was all I could do to keep my anger in check. I started muttering, as though talking to myself.

"Just being thrown in jail isn't a crime. If we can figure out the ant for crime then we can grasp the essence of crime. . . . God? Salvation? Love? Light? But Satan is the ant for God and I suppose that suffering would be the ant for salvation. Hate for love, darkness for light, evil for virtue. Crime and prayer, crime and regret, crime and confession, crime and . . . Ah, I give up. They're all synonyms. What is the ant for crime?"

"The opposite of crime is revenge. Sweet like revenge. I'm starving here. Go get me something to eat."

"Go get it yourself!" For what may very well have been the first time in my life, I roared in anger.

"Fine. I'll just wander downstairs and commit some crimes with Yoshi-chan. A hands-on experiment will reveal more than any amount of debate. The ant of crime is sweet beans. No, broad beans."

He was so drunk by then he could barely speak without slurring.

"Do what you like. Just get the hell out of here!"

"Crime and hunger, hunger and beans—no, they're synonyms," he continued to mutter nonsense as he clambered to his feet.

Crime and punishment. Dostoevsky. This thought grazed the edge of my consciousness and I gasped with sudden realization. What if we looked at Mr. Dost's *Crime and Punishment* not as synonyms, but reconfigured them as antonyms? Crime and punishment . . . Utterly at odds with one another, chalk and cheese.

Dost's crime and punishment as ants . . . Dost's fetid swamp, a pond teeming with algae, the very depths of chaos . . . Ah, I was on the verge of realization but no, still . . . It was then, just as these thoughts were racing through my head like the shadows of a spinning lantern . . .

"Hey! Terrible beans! Get down here!" Horiki was standing over me. His voice sounded strange, his pallor off. He'd just stumbled off downstairs but he was back already.

"What's wrong?"

There was a strange tension in the air as we went down the stairs to the second floor. Halfway down the next flight of stairs Horiki stopped.

"Look!" He whispered urgently, pointing.

The small window above my room was open and we could see inside. The light was on, two animals were inside.

I felt dizzy, my vision blurred. It's just what human beings do, that's all. No cause for surprise, I whispered to myself, gasping for breath. I stood rooted to the spot, forgetting even to go to Yoshiko's aid.

Horiki cleared his throat loudly. I fled, springing up the stairs to the roof where I threw myself down, face to the drizzling summer night. What I felt then was not rage, hatred, or even sadness but rather an overpowering terror. It was not the terror of a ghost in a graveyard. It was the terror of encountering a spirit, clad all in white, amid the towering cedars of a Shintō shrine. A ferocious, ancient terror that robbed me of speech. My hair began to turn gray that night. I lost confidence in everything. I was suspicious of everyone. I was forever alienated from all notions of hope, sympathy, or joy in the workings of the world. This was truly a decisive moment in my life. It was as though my head had been split open and, from that moment on, any interaction whatsoever with human beings caused that wound to throb.

"I feel bad for you but maybe now you'll know better. I'm not coming back here. This place . . . It's hell. But you should forgive Yoshi-chan. You're no prize yourself, after all. Well, I'm off."

Horiki was no fool. He wasn't one to linger when things grew awkward.

I sat up, drank the *shōchū*, crying bitterly. I thought I could go on weeping forever.

At some point Yoshiko had come up to the roof. She stood behind me, holding a dish heaped with broad beans, a vacant expression on her face.

"He said . . . he wouldn't do anything. . . ."

"No. Don't say anything. It's never occurred to you to doubt people. Sit down. Have some beans."

We sat next to one another, eating beans. Could it be that trust is a crime? He was a shopkeeper, a small, stupid man of about thirty who commissioned cartoons from me, always making a great show of reluctance when it came to paying me the few coins that were my fee.

The shopkeeper didn't dare come around again after that, but, for some reason, I found I hated Horiki even more than the shopkeeper. Horiki, who'd discovered them at it but, rather than coughing or clearing his throat to interrupt them, just left and came back up to the roof to tell me. On sleepless nights this hatred and rage had me writhing and groaning in my bed.

It was not a question of forgiving or not forgiving. Yoshiko had a gift for trusting people. She didn't know to be suspicious of them. Therein lies the tragedy.

I ask you, God. Is trust a crime?

It wasn't that Yoshiko had been defiled but that her trust had been violated. This caused me such unbearable pain I thought I couldn't go on living. For someone like me, mean and trembling, forever humoring those around him, whose ability to trust had already been irrevocably shattered, Yoshiko's pure and innocent trust was as clean and refreshing as a waterfall deep in the woods. In one night it had turned to filthy, yellow sewage. Do you see? Ever since that night Yoshiko trembled before even my slightest smile or frown.

If I called out to her she gave a start and looked around nervously. No matter how hard I tried to make her laugh, no matter how much I played the clown she always seemed to be quivering with fright. She started talking to me with excessive politeness.

Is innocent trust, in the end, the root of all crime?

I read every story I could find featuring wives who were violated. Yet, not one of them had been so cruelly violated as Yoshiko. There was nothing, not the slightest element of fiction about it. My suffering might have been eased somewhat had there been anything even faintly resembling love between Yoshiko and the shopkeeper, but, in the end, it came down to one summer night when Yoshiko trusted someone and that was all there was to it. And so my head seemed to shatter, my voice grew hoarse, my hair turned gray before its time, and Yoshiko trembled in fear the rest of her life. Most of the stories I read focused on whether or not the husband would forgive his wife's "deeds," but that wasn't such a terribly important point for me. Happy indeed, I thought, is the husband who has the right to decide whether or not to forgive. If he deems the offense unforgivable there's no need for a fuss, he simply divorces her out of hand and finds a new wife. Or, if he can't do that, he "forgives" her and endures. In either case, everything is arranged to suit the husband's feelings. That is, while it no doubt comes as quite a shock to the husband, in the end it is for all that nothing more than a "shock"—not something one returns to over and over again, endlessly, like the pounding of waves on the shore. It is, I thought, the kind of problem that, one way or the other, could be resolved by a husband's righteous anger. Yet, in my case, I possessed none of the rights of the husband, and the more I considered it, the more it seemed to me that everything was my fault. Far from being angry with her, I dared not utter the slightest word of reproach. Indeed, it was because she possessed such rare virtue that she had been violated. It was that virtue, that pure and innocent trust, long admired, that her husband had found so unutterably endearing.

Is innocent trust a crime?

Even that sole, saving virtue was now clouded with suspicion. Nothing made sense to me anymore. My only refuge was alcohol. I drank *shōchū* from the moment I got up, my features coarsened beyond recognition, several teeth fell out, my cartoons devolved into little more than pornography. No, I'll be honest. I'd started copying erotic prints and selling them in secret. I needed the money for *shōchū*. Whenever I looked at Yoshiko, trembling and too frightened to meet my gaze, I recalled how completely trusting she'd once been, and I couldn't help wondering if that little shopkeeper had been the only one. Maybe Horiki? Or maybe a complete stranger? Suspicion gave rise to suspicion, yet, still, I lacked the courage to come out and ask her directly. So I got drunk on *shōchū,* and, writhing in my usual terror and anxiety, I made timorous attempts at confronting her, plying her with contemptible leading questions. Like a fool, I alternated between joy and sorrow even as, on the surface, I continued to play the clown to the hilt. I subjected her to despicable, torturous, loving caresses, and then passed out, dead drunk.

Toward the end of that year I came home late one night, stinking drunk. I wanted a glass of sugar water but Yoshiko was already asleep, so I went to the kitchen and dug around for the sugar jar, but when I opened it I discovered that instead of sugar there was only a small, slender black box. I picked it up absently and was astonished when I saw the writing on the box. Most of the letters had been scratched off, probably with someone's fingernail, but the English writing remained. "DIAL."

Dial. I was drinking so much *shōchū* those days I'd stopped using sleeping pills, but, as I'd always been plagued with insomnia, I was familiar with most of the brands. And in that single box of Dial was certainly more than enough for a fatal dose. The seal was intact but she must've tried to erase the letters and then hid the box in the sugar jar because, some day, she'd want it and it would be there. Poor girl, unable to read the Roman alphabet, she'd only scratched part of the English writing off before deciding it was enough. (You have committed no crime.)

Careful not to make a sound, I filled a glass with water and, slowly breaking the seal on the box, I tipped its contents into my mouth and calmly drank the glass of water down in one go before turning out the lights and going to bed.

I slept like the dead for three days and nights. The doctor put it down as an accidental overdose so they were able to hold off reporting it to the police. Apparently the first thing I said upon regaining consciousness was that I wanted to go home. Where, precisely, I meant by "home" wasn't clear even to me, but they told me I broke down in tears after I said it.

The fog gradually lifted, and, opening my eyes, I saw Flounder, looking disgruntled, sitting by my pillow.

"Last time it was the end of the year too, you know. It's always the end of the year with him. The one time we're busiest, running around like mad. It's our health he's putting at risk with stunts like this."

He was talking to the Madam of the Kyōbashi bar.

"Madam?" I called out.

"Yes? What is it? Are you awake?" She looked down at me, her smiling face seeming almost to cover my own.

Tears streamed down my cheeks.

"Let me divorce Yoshiko." The words were out before I realized what I was saying.

I heard a faint sigh as she straightened.

It was then that I let slip something so truly outlandish, something so comical and so idiotic it defies description.

"I, I want to go someplace where there aren't any women."

Flounder reacted first, roaring with laughter. Madam began to giggle, and soon I too flushed and grinned wryly, tears still running down my cheeks.

"Yes indeed, a fine idea," Flounder said. His coarse laughter seemed to go on forever. "You should go someplace where there aren't any women. You fall to pieces when there are women around. No women—that's a fine idea."

Someplace without women. This silly, flippant wish would later be realized in the most dismal manner imaginable.

Yoshiko had somehow convinced herself that, in taking the pills, I'd been sacrificing myself for her, that I'd been taking her place. As a result she became even more timid, never smiling at anything I said, hardly speaking at all. It was too depressing at home, so I was forever going out, drowning myself in cheap liquor again. Ever since the Dial incident, though, I'd gone as thin as a rail. My arms and legs felt heavy and I fell behind in my cartoon work. Flounder left me some money when he came to see me at the hospital (he'd called it a "small gift from Shibuta" when he handed it over, acting for all the world as if it were coming out of his own pocket, but it seems that it too was from my brothers. Unlike when I ran away from his house, I saw through Flounder's play-acting now—if only vaguely—and when he started putting on airs I played my part too, pretending not to suspect a thing, muttering my meek thanks. There were times I almost understood why Flounder insisted on these convoluted deceptions and times I did not. It was all very strange to me), so I spontaneously decided to use it for a solitary tour of the hot springs in southern Izu. But I was unsuited for a leisurely trip to the spas. I grew inconsolable when I thought of Yoshiko, and the reflective state of mind you need to contemplate mountain landscapes eluded me entirely. I didn't bother changing into the quilted jacket provided by the inn, nor did I bother with the baths. Instead I rushed outside and, bursting into a grimy coffee shop, bathed myself in *shōchū* instead. By the time I went back to Tokyo, I was in even worse shape than when I'd left.

It had snowed heavily in Tokyo. I was stumbling about,

drunk, in one of the back alleys of Ginza, quietly singing the refrain, "How many hundreds of leagues from home," over and over again, kicking the tips of my shoes at the snow that had accumulated when I suddenly vomited. That was the first time I'd ever vomited blood. I'd made a giant rising sun flag in the snow. For a while I just squatted there, scooping up clean snow in both hands and washing my face with it as I wept.

> Whaaat narrow alley is thiiis?
> Whaaat narrow alley is thiiis?

The forlorn voice of a young girl singing the nursery rhyme seemed to drift out from the darkness, so faint I thought my ears might be playing tricks on me. Misery. The world had all sorts of miserable people—I doubt it would be much of an exaggeration to say it was filled with miserable people. Yet their misery was of the sort where they could unabashedly protest their misery to "society." "Society," in turn, immediately understood their protest and was sympathetic to it. My misery, on the other hand, was entirely the product of my own guilt, so there was nobody I could turn to. Should I venture even the most tentative of objections it wouldn't just be Flounder sneering at me, despairing at my nerve, but all of society as a whole. Was it simply that I, as the saying goes, thought "the whole world revolves around me"? Or was it the opposite? Was I too timid? I myself had no idea. I was nothing more than a lump of guilt, capable only of making myself ever more miserable, with absolutely no idea how to stop.

I stood up and my first thought was to get some sort of

medicine, so I went to the nearest pharmacy. My gaze met that of the lady of the shop. Instantly. She lifted her head, eyes widening as though bathed in a flash of light, standing rooted to the spot. Yet her eyes widened not in loathing or fear but rather in pleading, as though yearning for salvation. Ah, she is miserable too. I'm certain of it. Those who suffer misery can sense it in others. Just as this thought crossed my mind I saw her totter as she leaned heavily on a pair of crutches. I had to suppress my sudden urge to rush to her side. Tears spilled from my eyes as I gazed at her. Her large eyes began to overflow with tears as well.

That's all. Without a single word, I turned and left, stumbling back to my apartment. I had Yoshiko make me a glass of salt water and, drinking it down, went to bed without a word. The next morning I lied and said that I felt a cold coming on so I could spend the day in bed. By the time night fell, I had grown so anxious I could endure it no longer and I went back to the pharmacy, this time smiling as I explained my condition in detail and asked the woman for advice.

"You have to stop drinking."

She spoke familiarly, as though we were relatives.

"But I think I might be an alcoholic. Even now I want a drink."

"You mustn't. My husband got TB and drowned himself in liquor. Said it'd kill off the bacteria but it ended up killing him instead."

"I'm too frightened, I can't. I'm too scared."

"I'll give you some medicine. But you must stop drinking no matter what."

The woman (a widow with a son who'd gone to medical

school in Chiba or someplace like that but, as soon as he got accepted he came down with the same illness that killed his father and now he was on leave, convalescing in hospital. She had a bedridden father-in-law at home and one of her legs had been useless ever since she came down with polio when she was five) stumped around the shop on her crutches taking things from this shelf and that drawer as she gathered up various medicines for me.

> This one will replenish your blood.
> These are vitamin injections. The syringe is here.
> These are calcium supplements. Diastase to settle your stomach.

This one for this, that one for that—she went on, lovingly explaining five or six different kinds of medicines, but, in the end, even this miserable woman's love was too much for me. Finally, she said, deftly wrapping a small box, this is for when you can't take it anymore and absolutely must have a drink.

It was morphine.

She said it wouldn't be as bad as liquor, and I believed her. What's more, it had gotten to the point where even I had come to think there was something unclean about the way I drank. For the first time in a very long time I felt a sense of joy at the prospect of being able to escape from the Satan of liquor. So without any hesitation I promptly injected the morphine into my arm. Instantly, all my anxiety, irascibility, and timidity melted clean away. I was garrulous, cheerful. One shot of morphine and even my worries about my declining health vanished. I poured myself into my cartoons, coming up with ideas so odd and so amusing that I burst out laughing even as I drew.

I meant to limit myself to one injection a day but before long one became two and by the time two became four I couldn't work without it.

"You have to stop. If you get addicted . . . Well, that would be terrible."

When the woman said that I figured that I must already be well and truly addicted (I was extremely susceptible to the suggestions of others. Somehow I'd managed to convince myself of the odd notion that I was obliged to disappoint people. If someone handed me money and said, "You really shouldn't spend it but, being you, you'll probably spend it anyway," I felt that I *had* to spend the money, that it was my duty to disappoint them, and I would rush right out and spend every last coin), but the idea that I might be addicted only made me more anxious and this, in turn, caused me to crave the drug all the more.

"Please, I'm begging you. Just one more box. I'll pay what I owe you at the end of the month, I promise."

"It's not the bill that concerns me, you can pay that whenever you like. It's the police I'm worried about."

Ah, it seems I am doomed forever to have a cunning, gloomy, shadowy aura trailing about after me.

"You'll find a way to get around them. I'm begging you. Shall I give you a kiss?"

She blushed, and I saw my opening.

"Look, without the medicine I can't get any work done at all. It's like a stimulant."

"In that case you'd do better with a hormone injection."

"Don't make fun of me. If I can't drink then it's got to be the medicine. I can't work without either of them."

"But you mustn't drink."

"Right? And ever since I started taking the medicine I haven't touched a drop. Thanks to you I'm feeling much better. I'm not going to spend my whole life drawing lousy cartoons, you know. I'll stop drinking, get my health back, work hard, and one day I'll become a famous painter, you'll see. This is a critical time for me. Please, I'm begging you. Here, I'll give you a kiss."

At that the woman burst out laughing. "You're hopeless, you know that? Don't blame me if get addicted though."

She thumped across the floor with her crutches and took the drug from a shelf.

"I can't give you the whole box. You'll go through it in no time. You can have half."

"Stingy, aren't you? Still, it's better than nothing, I suppose."

I injected an ampule as soon as I got home.

"Doesn't it hurt?" Yoshiko asked timidly.

"'Course it hurts. But I've got no choice. If I'm going to get through all this work, I've got to do it, whether I like it or not. I'm a lot better these days, right? Now I've got work to do. Work, work, work." I chattered away cheerfully.

Once I even showed up in the dead of night, pounding on the shop door. When she came tottering out on crutches, still in her nightclothes, I grabbed her, kissing her, and pretending to cry.

Wordlessly, she handed me a box.

By the time I realized that the drug was just as vile as *shōchū*—no, even worse—I was a full-blown addict. I had truly reached the depths of degradation. Desperate for the drug, I'd started copying erotic prints again, and it wasn't long before the crippled woman and I began, quite literally, an ugly affair.

I want to die. Now more than ever, I want to die. There is no going back. There is nothing I can do. Nothing can help. I can only add more layers of shame. Dreams of bicycle rides and forest waterfalls are not for me. My lot is to lay one filthy, contemptible crime atop another, to suffer ever more violent anguish. I want to die. I have to die. Life itself is the root of all crime.

Near mad and consumed with these thoughts, I nevertheless continued to spend each day running back and forth between my room and the pharmacy.

The more I worked, the more I needed the drug, and before long I'd accumulated a terrifying debt. Whenever the lady from the pharmacy saw me tears welled up in her eyes even as they trickled down my cheeks.

Hell.

This was my last chance to escape from hell. If it fails, I thought, there is nothing left for me but a noose around my neck. Thus resolved, as though wagering everything on the existence of God, I wrote a long letter to Father. In it I confessed everything (except for the woman. Even I couldn't bring myself to write about that) about my current state.

The outcome was even worse than I had imagined. Days passed one after another yet no reply came. I grew restless and anxious and this, in turn, made me take even more of the drug.

Tonight, I secretly resolved, tonight I'll inject ten ampules and jump in the river. That very afternoon, as though possessed of the devil's own intuition, Flounder showed up, Horiki tagging along behind him.

"I hear you've been coughing up blood?"

Horiki sat cross-legged in front of me. So kind and gentle was his smile that I thought I'd never seen its like before. I was overwhelmed with gratitude and so overjoyed by his kindly smile I had to turn away lest they see the tears streaming down my cheeks. That one, gentle smile utterly destroyed me. I was buried alive.

I was put in a car. The most important thing is to get you to a hospital. We'll take care of everything else, Flounder urged quietly (so gentle were his words I could almost describe them as compassionate), and, as though all will and judgment of my own had vanished, I wept softly as I obeyed every command, the very soul of meekness. Yoshiko climbed in the car too, and the four of us jostled and swayed as we drove for what seemed a very long time. Just as the sky began to darken the car stopped at the entrance to a large hospital deep in a forest.

A sanatorium. I was certain of it.

A young doctor subjected me to a disconcertingly courteous, tender examination.

"Well, I think you should rest here for a little while," he said with an almost shy smile. Flounder, Horiki, and Yoshiko were to return home, leaving me there all on my own. As they turned to go, Yoshiko handed me a cloth bundle containing a change of clothes and then, wordlessly, held out the syringe and remaining ampules of morphine. It seems she really had believed me when I said it was just a stimulant.

"No, I don't need it anymore."

This was truly remarkable. I'm not exaggerating when I say that this solitary instance was the only time in my entire life I rejected something offered me. Mine was the misery of one who cannot say no. I was terrified that, should I refuse, an irreparable, eternal crack would snake through the both of us. Yet, at that instant, though half-mad with cravings, I refused the morphine without a second thought. Perhaps I'd been moved by Yoshiko's "divine ignorance." I wonder if my addiction did not cease at that precise moment.

After that the young doctor with the shy smile showed me to one wing of the hospital, and then I heard the lock clang shut. I was in a lunatic asylum.

I want to go someplace where there aren't any women. That careless remark, uttered after the Dial incident, had been, it seems, realized in the most peculiar manner. My wing of the hospital held only men who were insane. Even the nurses were men. Not a single woman to be seen.

I was no longer a mere criminal. I was mad. But no, I certainly wasn't insane or anything like it. I'd never, not for a moment, gone mad. Ah, but I suppose that's the sort of thing a lunatic would say. I suppose that if they put you in this hospital it means you're crazy, and if they don't, it means you're normal.

I ask you, God. Is it a crime not to resist?

I was moved to tears by Horiki's strangely beautiful smile, I abandoned all judgment and resistance, I got in the car, I was brought here, I became a lunatic. Even were I to leave right now, I would still be branded a lunatic. No. Not a lunatic. A cripple.

A human, failed.

I had, utterly and completely, ceased to be human.

When I arrived it was early summer, and, peering through the bars of my window, I could see the red blossoms of lilies floating atop the small pond in the hospital garden. Three months later the cosmos were starting to bloom, and, my eldest brother, with Flounder in tow, appeared out of the blue to get me out. Father had died of a gastric ulcer at the end of last month. We don't care about your past. We don't want you to worry about money. You don't have to do anything. In exchange, you have to leave everything, get out of Tokyo right away, and go to the countryside to recover. We know you still have unfinished business in Tokyo but Shibuta has already taken care of most of the loose ends so you don't need to worry about it. My brother spoke in his characteristically tense, somber manner.

I could almost see the mountains and rivers of my hometown floating before my eyes. I gave a weak nod.

Truly, a cripple.

My last pillar crumbled when I heard that Father was dead. He was no more. That presence, comforting and terrifying, had always been with me. Gone. It was as though the vessel of anguish had run dry. I even wondered if it was because of Father that this vessel had weighed so heavily upon me. All motivation fled me. I'd lost even the ability to suffer.

My brother was true to his word and did all that he promised. Four or five hours south of my hometown by train there is a hot springs region near the sea that is unusually warm for northeast Japan. He bought me a house on the outskirts of a small village there. It had five rooms, crumbling walls, and pillars chewed away by insects. It was so dilapidated as to be almost beyond repair. He also provided me with a servant, an ugly woman of almost sixty years with horrible rust-colored hair.

I've been here a little more than three years now and have

been subjected to any number of odd violations by that old servant, Tetsu. Sometimes we argue like an old married couple. Sometimes my lung disease worsens, sometimes it improves. I grow thinner and I grow fatter. Sometimes I cough up blood. Yesterday I sent Tetsu to the pharmacy to buy me a box of Carmotine, my usual sedative. The box she brought back was different from the usual one, but I didn't take particular note of it. Though I took ten tablets before going to bed I still didn't feel at all sleepy. Just as I started to wonder at this, my stomach suddenly started rumbling, and, rushing to the toilet, I suffered a terrible attack of diarrhea. I had to run to the toilet three more times that night. Growing suspicious, I looked at the box more carefully and saw that it was actually Crapotine, a laxative.

I lay flat on my back in bed, a hot water bottle atop my stomach, thinking about what I would say to Tetsu.

"Look here, this isn't Carmotine at all—it's Crapotine!" But before I could go any further, I started to giggle. I guess, in the end, "cripple" is a comic noun. The cripple tries to sleep but takes a laxative instead. To top it off, the laxative is called "Crapotine."

I am beyond joy or misery now.

All things pass.

That is the only truth I have encountered in all the days I've spent in this cold hell of a world of so-called "humans."

All things pass.

I will be twenty-seven years old this year. My hair has turned gray and most people would say I look over forty.

EPILOGUE

I never actually met the madman who composed these journals. I do, however, have a passing acquaintance with the woman described as "the Madam of the Kyōbashi bar." She is a small woman with a sallow complexion. She has narrow, pinched eyes, a prominent nose, and a general steeliness about her associated less with a "beautiful woman" than, perhaps, with a "handsome youth." The Tokyo described in the journals appears to be mainly that of 1930 to 1932, but since my friend didn't take me to the Kyōbashi bar for highballs until around the time "militarists" started parading about openly—1935 or so—I never had the opportunity to meet the author who wrote these pages.

It was this past February when I went to pay a visit on an acquaintance who had evacuated Tokyo for the city of Funabashi, just to the east in Chiba Prefecture. He was a friend from my university days and now holds a post lecturing at a women's college. The purpose of my visit was to ask his assistance with arrangements surrounding the marriage of one of my relatives. As Funabashi was near the shore, I thought I might as well get some fresh seafood while I was there and treat my family to a feast. Thus, backpack slung across my shoulders, I set out.

Funabashi is a fairly large city overlooking the muddy sea. My friend's house was in a newer part of the city, and, though

I showed the locals his address and asked directions, nobody seemed to know quite where it was. Not only was I getting cold, the straps of my backpack were digging into my shoulders, and so, drawn by the sound of classical music, I opened the door to a coffee shop.

The woman running the shop looked familiar and, inquiring, I discovered she was none other than the Madam of that tiny Kyōbashi bar of some ten years ago. She apparently recognized me too and we greeted one another, laughing with exaggerated surprise. Dispensing with the all-too-familiar stories of air raids burning us out of house and home, we seemed to grow almost boastful as we talked.

"Look at you! You haven't changed at all!"

"Nonsense. I'm an old lady with aching bones now. You're as young as ever, though!"

"I wish I were. I've got three kids now. They're the reason I'm out here today—foraging for food."

We continued in this vein for a little while, exchanging the sort of pleasantries you'd expect to hear from two companions meeting after a long absence. We were speaking of mutual acquaintances and what had become of them when she suddenly grew serious and asked me if I knew Yō-chan. When I told her I didn't she went into the back and returned with three notebooks and three photographs.

"They might give you ideas for a novel," she said, handing them to me.

Normally I find it impossible to write about material that someone else has foisted on me, and I was about to hand the journals back when the photos caught my eye (I describe these very peculiar photos in the preface), so I took the journals and told her I would stop by again on my way home. I asked if she knew the lecturer at the woman's college at such and such an address and it turned out that she did, being a newly established resident herself. He lived just down the street and even stopped by the coffee shop from time to time.

That night my friend and I shared what little liquor he had on hand, and he invited me to spend the night. I stayed up the whole time, absorbed in the journals.

Though they describe events of some time ago, I was certain they would be of great interest to readers even today. Rather than make a botch of things by trying to rewrite them myself I thought it better by far to find a magazine willing to publish them as they were.

The only gifts I'd been able to find for my children were dried seafood so, settling my pack on my shoulders, I left my friend's house and stopped in at the coffee shop again.

"It was nice seeing you again yesterday. By the way, may I hold on to these notebooks a little while longer?" I said, getting straight to the point.

"Of course. Please do."

"Is he still alive? The man who wrote them?"

"Well now, I'm afraid I have no idea. The journals and photos were sent to my old place in Kyōbashi about ten years ago. It must have been Yō-chan who sent them but there was no return address, not even a name. It's a wonder they weren't lost along with everything else in the air raids. It was only the other day that I read them all the way through."

"Did you cry?"

"Cry? No, I didn't cry. Only . . . well, it's just no good. There's nothing you can do when someone gets like that."

"If that was ten years ago, I suppose he might've died by now. He must've sent them by way of thanking you. No doubt he exaggerated a bit here and there but it sounds like you went through a lot as well. If it's all true and I were his friend, I suppose I would've been tempted to take him to an asylum too."

"It's all his father's fault," she said absently. "The Yō-chan I knew was kind and so gentle. If only he didn't drink—no, even when he did drink . . . He was such a good boy. An angel."

TRANSLATOR'S AFTERWORD

Readers of a translation naturally come to the text with a perspective and leave it with an experience very different from those of native speakers who read the work in its original language. Affecting any translation of Japanese into English, in addition to the not inconsiderable linguistic gap separating the two languages, there are the obvious differences in culture and context. Dazai's writings in general, and *A Shameful Life* (*Ningen shikkaku*, 1948) in particular, are perhaps more deeply affected by these differences than many other novels.

This is not to say that Dazai's writing cannot be enjoyed without knowledge of Japanese, without knowledge of prewar, wartime, and postwar Japan, or without knowledge of Dazai himself. On the contrary, even as the original stands quite firmly on its own two feet, so, too, do I hope that the translation is sufficient unto itself and that a reader knowing nothing of Japan whatsoever can still take something meaningful away from it. Indeed, the ability to approach the novel *tabula rasa* is, in this case, an experience that few Japanese readers can enjoy. Even those who are not enthusiastic consumers of literature will know something of Dazai's life and exploits, for he is nearly as infamous in Japan as he is famous. The purpose of this Afterword, then, is to fill in some of those gaps in awareness and to provide non-Japanese readers with a better understanding of the context in which the novel was written and in which it was—and continues to be—read in Japan today. If you have skipped to this Afterword before reading the novel and would like to approach it first without preconceptions—or with different preconceptions—you would do well to start it now, returning here only after you are done.

In order to better understand Dazai's work, it is important to understand the complex relationship between his writings and the genre of the "I-novel" or, in Japanese, the *shishōsetsu* or *watakushi-shōsetsu*. The I-novel emerged as a dominant force in Japanese letters during the early twentieth century, and only a very few Japanese writers of the time managed to resist its lure entirely, whether they were devoted practitioners of the form or not.[1] The I-novel was typically contrasted to the *honkaku shōsetsu*—the "authentic novel," the ideal manifestation of which one Japanese critic located in Tolstoy's *Anna Karenina*.[2] A great deal of ink was expended by critics and authors at the time in debate over which of the two forms embodied the true essence of literary expression.

Nakamura Murao, a proponent of the authentic novel, defined it as a strictly objective, third-person novel that "does not express the author's state of mind or feelings but instead represents his attitude toward life through the depiction of certain

1   Edward Fowler, *The Rhetoric of Confession: Shishōsetsu in Early Twentieth Century Japanese Fiction* (Los Angeles: University of California Press, 1988), xvi.

2   Nakamura Murao makes this claim in his 1924 essay, "Honkaku shōsetsu to shinkyō shōsetsu to." Cited in Ogasawara Masaru, "Honkaku shōsetsu," in *Nihon kindai bungaku jiten*, ed. Odagiri Susumu (Tokyo: Kodansha, 1977), 4:486.

characters and their lives."[3] The authentic novel is one in which the figure of the author is actively concealed and its ". . . interest and significance . . . does not lie in who wrote it but in 'what is written.'"[4]

In contrast, the I-novel was seen by many as meaningful ". . . only insofar as it illuminates the life [of the author]."[5] Disparaging voices such as Nakamura's aside, the I-novel had no shortage of enthusiastic adherents, and for many years the bulk of the Japanese literary establishment considered it to be the epitome of "pure" literary expression. "Authentic" novels with their focus on plot-driven narratives (such as Tolstoy's) were dismissed as "vulgar" fiction.[6] According to novelist, playwright, and poet Kume Masao (1891–1952), only the I-novel, with its relentless introspection, constituted the ". . . root, the true path, and the essence" of art.[7]

The I-novel and the authentic novel, then, differed not only in content—one focused on the life of the author and the other on "attitudes toward life"—they also differed significantly in form. Concerned with representing the thoughts, feelings, and anxieties of the author/narrator/protagonist with the greatest possible fidelity, I-novel narratives were not overly concerned with plot development or with showing how a character

---

3 Nakamura Murao, "Honkaku shōsetsu to shinkyō shōsetsu to," cited in Tomi Suzuki, *Narrating the Self: Fictions of Japanese Modernity* (Stanford: Stanford University Press, 1996), 49.

4 Ibid., 49.

5 Fowler, *The Rhetoric of Confession*, xviii.

6 Ogasawara Masaru, "Shinkyō shōsetsu," in *Nihon kindai bungaku jiten*, ed. Odagiri Susumu (Tokyo: Kodansha, 1977), 4:223.

7 Cited in Ino Kenji, "Watakushi shōsetsu," *Nihon kindai bungaku jiten,* ed. Odagiri Susumu (Tokyo: Kodansha, 1977), 4:540.

transforms or overcomes a particular problem. I-novels have, in terms of plot at least, no obvious direction or "purpose." In this the I-novel differs not only from the authentic novel but also from more conventional autobiography. As Phyllis Lyons notes in her excellent study on Dazai, his writings differ from autobiography in that he does not ". . . explain *why* something happened and what its effects were . . . but only shows *that* things happen."[8] The same could be said of most I-novels. They are concerned not with the "why," or even the "how," so much as they are with the "what." The resultant text, with its lack of a clearly defined, linear plot, can often be disorienting to the unfamiliar reader.

Writers of the I-novel often employed a "confessional" form of writing to depict and define the self with unflinching honesty, regardless of the harm it might do them. One of the foremost practitioners of the art, Shimazaki Tōson (1872–1943), was willing to sacrifice not only himself at the altar of pure literature but his niece as well when he detailed his affair with her in his novel *New Life* (*Shinsei*, 1918–19). Though Tōson was roundly criticized for his moral failings as well as the perceived crudity of trying to exploit the situation, the element of confession—though usually far less dramatic—was key to many I-novels. Not to lure in readers with salacious stories, or at least not primarily to lure in readers, but rather to achieve a "realistic" portrayal of the author/narrator/protagonist. No clear picture of the mind and self of the author could emerge unless everything—including the unsavory—was put on display. More than the mode of narration,

---

8   Phyllis Lyons, *The Saga of Dazai Osamu: A Critical Study with Translations* (Stanford: Stanford University Press, 1985), 82.

Kume Masao states, it was the way "the author exposes himself most directly" that defined the I-novel.[9]

Much of Dazai's writing can be said to fall into the camp of the I-novel, and that is one reason talking about Dazai can be so complicated. That is, much of what we know about the man, we know from his own writings. Furthermore, we know that these writings are not always strictly accurate. In her book *The Saga of Dazai Osamu*, Lyons addresses this dilemma by defining Dazai himself as a literary character, as a persona created, developed, and defined through and across his own writings. Of Dazai's story "Recollections" (*Omoide*, 1933), Lyons says it is ". . . a biography, but that of a literary character that Dazai made of himself."[10] Viewed from this perspective, then, the question of factual accuracy is ". . . not only meaningless, . . . but is irrelevant."[11] That is, Tsushima Shūji—for whom Dazai Osamu was a pen name—created the public, literary persona of Dazai Osamu and then proceeded to write the story, or the saga, of that literary persona's life. This saga would necessarily diverge from the lived reality of Tsushima Shūji as experiences are shaped into a coherent narrative.

The purpose of Dazai's writings is to "tell the tale," as Lyons puts it, and to give life to the literary character of "Dazai Osamu," not simply to record the bald facts of that life. Yet the facts are not irrelevant, either. Interrogated for his participation in illegal communist activities, investigated for aiding a suicide, attempting

---

9 Cited in Matthew Fraleigh, "Terms of Understanding: The Shōsetsu According to Tayama Katai," *Monumenta Nipponica* 58, no. 1 (Spring 2003): 46.

10 Lyons, *The Saga of Dazai Osamu*, 79.

11 Ibid., 81.

suicide multiple times, embroiled in vitriolic "debates" with leading literary figures, addicted to alcohol and opiates, and pursuing affairs with various mistresses, Dazai generated scandals that put him very much in the public eye. His writings are thus necessarily engaged with the facts of his life even when they "misrepresent" them. So well known are elements of Dazai's life that even when his writings diverge from fact, they effectively end up highlighting those facts. At such times a reader familiar with Dazai's exploits cannot help but stop and think, "But that's not what *really* happened." Dazai, too, would have been keenly aware of this, and this tension between "fact" and "fiction" is, I believe, a crucial component of *A Shameful Life*.

In *Ningen shikkaku*, whose title I have translated as "A Shameful Life" but which might be more literally rendered as "a failed human" or as "a disqualified human," Dazai creates a work that, with a remarkable degree of mastery, manages to blend the form, feel, and content of the confessional I-novel with the narrative structure and character development of more conventional fiction. Dazai draws on events from his own life but manipulates, alters, and distills them as he pours them into the vessel that is his protagonist, Ōba Yōzō.

***

Tsushima Shūji, who adopted the pen name Dazai Osamu (among others), was born on June 19, 1909, in the small town of Kanagi-mura, now called Goshogawara, on the Tsugaru Peninsula at the northern tip of Japan's main island, Honshū. He was the second youngest of seven sons and four daughters born to father Gen'emon and mother Tane. Gen'emon, as the head of one of the most prominent landowning families in Aomori Prefecture, also served as a representative in local and national parliaments, beginning a tradition of political service among the Tsushima family that continues to this day with Shūji's grandson, Tsushima Jun, serving his third term in the House of Representatives at the time of this writing.

As scholars have frequently noted, and as he himself frequently describes in his writings, Shūji had something of a confusing childhood. His mother, Tane, was often ill, and for the first few years of his life he was raised primarily by his aunt, Kiye, and her maid, Take. Both left when Shūji was six, Kiye to live with her newly married daughter and Take, newly married herself, to live with her husband. This sudden loss quite understandably left Shūji feeling abandoned, alone, and confused.

A bright child, Shūji began to show signs of literary talent in middle school where, like Yōzō in *A Shameful Life*, he penned stories designed to entertain his peers. One of his works, a story entitled, "Hanako-san," reputedly made his classmates laugh so hard that tears ran down their faces.[12]

Unlike the events that befall Yōzō in *A Shameful Life*, however, Shūji's father dies and his dour eldest brother, Bunji (1898–1973), takes over as head of household in 1923, the same year that Shūji enters middle school. When he goes on to Hirosaki Higher School (roughly equivalent to college in the new educational system), Shūji begins to study *gidayū*, a form of narrative chanting that accompanies *jōruri* (traditional Japanese

---

12 Usui Yoshimi, "Dazai Osamu," in *Nihon kindai bungaku jiten*, ed. Odagiri Susumu (Tokyo: Kodansha, 1977), 2:331.

puppet theater). He also awakens to the pleasures of drink and dissipation and begins an ill-fated affair with a geisha, Koyama Hatsuyo (1912–44). He continues to pursue his writing, founding and editing a coterie literary magazine, *Saibō bungei* ("Cell Literature"). It is during this time that he becomes acquainted with, and involved in, illegal communist activities. In 1929, in his third year at Hirosaki Higher School, Shūji makes his first known attempt at suicide, using the same sleeping medicine, Carmotine, that Yōzō's ill-mannered servant "accidentally" replaces with a laxative at the end of the novel.

The year 1930 is a busy one for Shūji. He enters the French Literature Department at Tokyo Imperial University despite not speaking a word of the language. He meets Ibuse Masuji (1898–1993), a writer whom Shūji had long admired and the man who would become his literary mentor. He also becomes increasingly involved in illegal political activities. Amid all of this, he helps Hatsuyo escape from her contract and brings her to live with him in Tokyo. Shūji's pursuit of a geisha was, of course, a terrible scandal for a household as prominent as the Tsushimas'—it is almost as embarrassing as his ties to communism. Shūji's elder brother Bunji has already become a prominent local politician in his own right, and he tries, to no avail, to persuade Shūji to give the girl up. In the end it is decided that she will stay with him. Shūji continues to receive a generous stipend while he continues his education. In exchange, all other ties between Shūji and his family are severed. Apparently pushed to his limits, Shūji tries to kill himself for the second time. Echoing the story of Tsuneko, in late November of 1930 Shūji attempts suicide with Tanabe Shimeko (1912–30), a waitress he's only just met at a Ginza café. As in the novel, Shimeko dies but Shūji is saved.

After escaping potential prosecution for abetting a suicide—no doubt thanks to his family's intervention—and recovering from the attempt, Shūji marries Hatsuyo, and the two set up house in a small apartment, reminiscent of Yōzō and Yoshiko and their tiny apartment in Tsukiji. This is not a happy beginning marked by domestic bliss, however, and Dazai describes it as ". . . a shameless, imbecilic time. I scarcely showed up at school at all, of course, I abhorred all effort, and spent my time lying around watching H[atsuyo] indifferently. It was crazy. I did nothing."[13] Unlike Yōzō, Shūji has an involvement in leftist activities that is no mere joke, at least not in terms of the consequences. Nor is he as skillful as Yōzō at evading the notice of the police. Shūji and Hatsuyo are forced to move house, renting apartments under assumed names, as the police search for them. In 1932 he is twice summoned by authorities for questioning about his links to illegal political activities, though he is released both times. It is also around this time that his image of Hatsuyo is irreparably shattered. Just as Yōzō despairs when Yoshiko's "pure and innocent trust" is transformed overnight into "filthy, yellow sewage," he discovers that Hatsuyo is not the "pure," inexperienced girl he thought he'd married.

After another suicide attempt in 1935, a failed hanging, Shūji falls seriously ill with appendicitis and not long thereafter becomes addicted to the oxycodeine-based painkiller Pavinal, first prescribed to treat pain related to post-operative complications.

---

13 Cited in Lyons, *The Saga of Dazai Osamu*, 32.

His mental and physical health, never good, deteriorate further, and in late 1936 he is admitted to a mental hospital for a month to break his addiction to the drug. While he is hospitalized, Hatsuyo has an affair with one of Shūji's friends. When Shūji discovers this in 1937, he and Hatsuyo go to a hot spring and attempt double suicide using Carmotine. The attempt fails, and the couple separate shortly thereafter.

The following year, mentor Ibuse Masuji introduces Shūji to Ishihara Michiko (1912–97) and in January of 1939 they marry. Not unlike Yōzō's life immediately after his marriage to Yoshiko, this marks a productive and relatively optimistic time in Shūji's life. His renown grows, his stories are published more widely, and he begins to accumulate prizes and awards. It is also at this time that he pens his most widely read and beloved work, "Hashire melosu" ("Run, Melos!," 1940). Shūji's lung ailment exempts him from active service during the war, and he manages to achieve something of a rapprochement with his family in Aomori, beginning with two visits to see his mother, who is ill and dies shortly after the second visit in 1942. He makes additional visits in 1944, when he is commissioned to write a "travel diary"–published in November of 1944 as *Tsugaru*, and again in 1945, when he and his family evacuate to Aomori to escape the bombings that are devastating most of Japan's urban centers.

Shūji does not move back to Tokyo until late 1946, and shortly afterward his life once again takes a decided turn for the worse. He is drinking heavily, coughing blood as a result of his tuberculosis, and has become embroiled in affairs with two different women–fathering a child with one of them and ultimately committing suicide with the other. It is also a time when he writes his two most famous and most enduring novels, *The Setting Sun* (*Shayō*, 1947) and *A Shameful Life* (*Ningen shikkaku*, 1948).

It is not surprising that critics have seen in these two grim novels a reflection of the despair that gripped Japan in the aftermath of its defeat in 1945. Its economy and urban centers have been demolished or, in the case of Hiroshima and Nagasaki, completely obliterated. Millions of Japanese citizens killed and died for naught. John Dower identifies this condition of *kyodatsu* or "exhaustion and despair," a condition that accompanied the overall "psychic collapse" of the nation's people after its defeat.[14] Of course, in *A Shameful Life* the only mention of the war appears in the Epilogue when—in a scene that would've been very familiar to urban readers at the time—the "discoverer" of the journals heads to Funabashi both to meet a friend and to forage for scarce food to feed his family. However, the bleak despair felt by the protagonist, the hopelessness and the deep distrust of everything and everyone that colors every aspect of the narrative, would likely have resonated particularly strongly with the postwar Japanese readership.

On June 13 Shūji and one of his lovers, Yamazaki Tomie (1919–48) jump into a nearby river, leaving unfinished his last work, *Good Bye* (*Guddo-bai*, 1948)—a comical story in which a man tries to break with his many mistresses. Their bodies aren't recovered until June 19, what would have been Shūji's

---

14 John Dower, *Embracing Defeat: Japan in the Wake of World War II* (New York: W. W. Norton, 1999), 88–89.

thirty-ninth birthday. The complete version of *A Shameful Life* appears in print a little over a month later.

***

As one might expect, critics and scholars have sought answers for Shūji's death in Dazai's literature. "Why did he die? The key to solving this riddle is doubtless to be found concealed in his writings from 'Recollections' to *A Shameful Life*," one scholar writes.[15] Lyons sees Dazai's writings as an extended suicide note. With the completion of *A Shameful Life*, she says, that note had come to an end. "There were no words for the next step. The suicide note was done. The period had finally been struck."[16]

There is, of course, no way to know for certain why Tsushima Shūji killed himself. The only person who might have been able to answer that question is dead. Clearly he was in ill-health, mentally and physically, and he had painted himself into something of a corner with various escapades in his personal life, though this was nothing new. Shūji had, after all, been involved in one scandal or another for much of his adult life. Did he truly kill himself because he had completed the "saga" of that literary persona, Dazai Osamu? After *A Shameful Life*, was there really nothing left to be said?

As noted earlier, Tsushima Shūji and Dazai Osamu are similar, yet distinct, beings. The latter can be seen as the "literary persona" partly lived and partly created by Tsushima Shūji. It is difficult, if not impossible, to draw a clear line demarcating the

---

15 Usui Yoshimi, "Dazai Osamu," 2:332.

16 Lyons, *The Saga of Dazai Osamu*, 186.

two as much of what we know (or think we know) about Shūji comes to us through the medium of his writings. As we see in the brief biography above, Yōzō, too, differs from Dazai, who, in turn, differs from Shūji. Despite the differences between them, it is a rare reader who can resist the impulse to try to "reverse engineer" the novel, discovering in Yoshiko composites of Hatsuyo and Michiko, finding Shigeko in Tsuneko, noting the similarities in upbringing, family, and so on. The intimate tone of the narrative and the form and conventions of the "I-novel" conspire to encourage such a reading.

It is here that the central irony of the text reveals itself. On the one hand, *A Shameful Life* is a novel that begs, if not demands, that the reader make the obvious connections leading from Yōzō to Dazai and thence to Shūji. Through his journals, Yōzō ostensibly provides the reader with an unfiltered, utterly candid window into his mind, a view that he says he has assiduously concealed from anyone and everyone throughout his life. The authenticity and immediacy of the narrative is emphasized further by the structure of the novel. That is, it is "framed" as three private journals that were sent, anonymously, to an acquaintance. It is only after they are handed to a writer that they are put before the public. Thus, not only were they *not* written for public display, the mediator—the writer who publishes them—makes a point of stating that he has not in any way altered the journals, further emphasizing their authenticity.

Yet, even as the novel presents itself as an unmediated window into the mind of Yōzō, and by extension Dazai and Shūji, it actively undermines that narrative. The journals themselves, after all, tell us time and again that the protagonist is "incapable of telling a single word of truth." This message is reinforced throughout the novel. Yōzō has, he tells us, "no faith whatsoever in the language of human beings." He believes that all people, himself included, "spend their entire lives deceiving and lying to one another." Yōzō's writings are portrayed as "nothing more than a simple form of clowning," and his cartoons—his primary artistic vehicle, just as writing is Dazai's—are simply a way to earn enough money to buy booze and cigarettes. The only "true" art he has created and the only "true" depictions of himself are located in his "monster paintings"—concealed from all but the halfwit Takeichi and paintings that, before long, are lost even to himself.

What are we to believe? It is akin to the Liar's Paradox. Do we believe that Yōzō is, as he says, incapable of telling the truth? Or do we believe that the journal (in which he says that he is incapable of telling the truth) is true? Or is he *only* telling the truth to the intended reader, presumably the Madam of the Kyōbashi bar, since that is the person he sent the journals to—and not to anyone else? Yet the novel, unlike the journals, is not private correspondence or an extended diary. It is, quite clearly, written for public consumption. It is just as clearly intended to allude to, if not directly chronicle, elements of Dazai's life and, through them, events in Shūji's life. Is it still, at this point, an unmediated window into the author's mind? Or has it become yet another mask?

Yōzō says that he was ". . . ignored when I was serious and only when I was clowning and deceiving . . . did my words seem to carry a ring of truth." Perhaps his words, in this context at least, are true. His words are certainly ignored by the Madam of the Kyōbashi bar. Despite having read the journals, she dismisses them out of hand. "It was all his father's fault," she claims. The Yōzō she knew, she says, "was an angel."

As readers, we risk falling into a similar trap. We risk seeing only half of the novel, just as the Madam has only seen half of Yōzō. We risk seeing in this novel the story of Dazai Osamu and, through him, the story of Tsushima Shūji. We risk looking for answers to such questions as why Tsushima Shūji committed suicide with Yamazaki Tomie. Yet in doing so we also ignore the overarching message of the novel. The impossibility of knowing another. That is, the impossibility of understanding and the impossibility of being understood.

Tsushima Shūji's suicide, coming so soon after completion of the manuscript and in a manner so similar to one described in the novel, cannot but have had a tremendous impact on the work's reception. It would have been all but impossible for people at the time to read the work without searching for clues or insights into the mind of Tsushima Shūji. Of course, it is this very same suicide that also made it impossible for the mind of Tsushima Shūji to ever be known. Here, too, then, are echoes of Yōzō and his journals. Both novel and journals are delivered to the reader only after the author had been irrevocably removed from the stage, making it impossible for us ever to know for certain where the truth lies. Perhaps this is the source of the novel's enduring appeal. Caught like the kite entangled in the wires outside of Shizuko's apartment, both Yōzō and the novel twist and writhe, trapped between the terror and desire of being understood, between the need to confess and the irresistible impulse to lie.

NOTE ON THE CURRENT TRANSLATION

Why? That was the first question asked when I proposed a new English-language translation of Osamu Dazai's masterpiece, *Ningen shikkaku*. After all, Donald Keene translated the novel (published under the title *No Longer Human*) over fifty years ago. It is still in print, and it sells well. Keene is, indisputably, one of the most important translators of Japanese literature into English, and this new translation is certainly not intended as a criticism of his work. In a way it is a product of Keene's work, as it is through Keene's translations that I first came to know, and eventually to love, Japanese literature. For that I owe him and the other incredibly prolific translators of his generation a tremendous debt. I am very cognizant of this debt.

Despite the obviousness of the question, the first time I was asked, "Why?" I had to struggle for an answer. This translation was not so much as planned as it was a somewhat self-indulgent accident. I had read the novel—in Keene's translation—some decades ago, and, not being a terribly sensitive reader at the time, I had put it down and didn't willingly go back to Dazai. It wasn't my cup of tea, or so I thought. A few years ago, however, students in my Japanese literature reading group asked for something a bit more demanding than what we had been reading, so I printed out a few pages of *Ningen shikkaku* from the

Aozora Bunko edition. I was immediately struck by Dazai's vivid, wandering, shifting, endless, labyrinthine sentences. How in the world does one translate something like this? Our reading group became translation practice sessions with a graduate student over beers at the Wig & Pen. The novel gradually turned into something of an obsession with me, and a few years and many, many drafts later, the translation was finished. Only then, with a completed manuscript, did I consider the question "Why?"

Each translation is an interpretation. For me, that is the most compelling answer to the question "Why?" Each translation, if successful, is a distillation of the translator's understanding of the work. It is the result of hundreds and thousands of decisions, large and small. The cumulative effect of these choices is enormous. Naturally, one cannot (or should not) choose to interpret the word "shoes" as the word "tiger," and in that respect the translator is bound in ways that the author is not. Yet, when translating between languages that are very different—and it is difficult to imagine two languages less alike than Japanese and English—the translator's interpretation plays an enormous role in the translation process.

All conscientious literary translators seek to stay true to the original. But what *is* the "original"? If a text has as many meanings as it does readers, how much truer does that hold in translating? What is the text trying to achieve in a certain passage? What impact does a particular expression, a particular phrasing, a particular structure have on the reader? What impact did it have on a Japanese reader in 1948? How does one recreate that for an English-language reader seventy years later? This is why we see—and *should* see—multiple translations of works worthy of the attention. Each translation enables us to see different elements of the original.

This translation is my attempt to answer the questions above as best I can. After finishing my translation, I reread Keene's version for the first time in many years. My answers, I think, differ significantly from Keene's answers. I do not say that they are better or worse than Keene's—they are simply different. After all, this is literature, not mathematics.

In my translation, and in my interpretation, of the text I have tried to emphasize Yōzō's voice. The intimacy and directness of that voice are, I believe, central to the novel. I have attempted to convey a voice that will pull the reader, effortlessly, into Yōzō's heart and mind—or at least as much of the heart and mind Yōzō decides to reveal.

At the same time, I have also tried to avoid "editing" Dazai's novel, even when doing so might have made it easier for me to convey the voice that I think is so critical to the text. Where Dazai is inconsistent or confusing in the original, I have tried to replicate this in the English. I have tried to retain cultural particularities even when they do not have a ready English equivalent. Where Dazai uses Japanese translations of foreign poems, I translated the Japanese translations Dazai used rather than using the originals. The result is perhaps less graceful in places, but I believe it to be truer to the original. Though I was sorely tempted, I chose not to use footnotes to explain the various references to poems, literary journals, and so on that litter the work. In the end I think that the benefit of these notes, of interest to only a small number of readers, did not justify the disruption in the narrative that they would cause.

Beyond providing a different interpretation of the novel, I hope that this translation will help to renew interest in Dazai and to encourage readers to explore his works more widely—and in different translations. He is truly one of the great writers of twentieth-century Japan.

Acknowledgments

I would like to acknowledge the support and help of people without whom this translation would not exist. Meredith McKinney was kind enough to read drafts of the translation. I am grateful, too, to Orion Lethbridge, one of the original reading group members, a translation practice participant, and a thoughtful reader of drafts. I am very grateful to the University of Chicago's Center for East Asian Studies Committee on Japanese Studies for supporting my translation by selecting it for the William F. Sibley Memorial Subvention Award. I would like to thank the staff of Stone Bridge Press for all of their work on behalf of the translation. Peter Goodman's painstaking copyediting of the translation, in particular, was invaluable. I would also, of course, like to thank my wife Miyako for her support, advice, encouragement, and superhuman patience.

—MG

DAZAI OSAMU (1909–48) retains an enormous following in Japan today and is as famous for his darkly introspective novels as for the light-hearted children's stories that are a staple of many Japanese textbooks. Son of a wealthy family in northern Japan, Dazai was a top student who showed an early penchant for literary writing. He led a troubled, unstable life and suffered from drug abuse and alcoholism; he attempted suicide and had numerous affairs, even as his literary fame grew. *A Shameful Life (Ningen shikkaku)*, is said to be a close approximation of his lifestyle and struggles. Shortly after its publication in 1948, Dazai and his lover drowned themselves in the Tamagawa Canal in western Tokyo.

MARK GIBEAU is a literary translator and scholar of postwar Japanese literature. His previous translations include fiction by Kawabata Yasunari, Tanizaki Jun'ichirō, Yamamoto Shūgorō, Tayama Sakumi, Kakuta Mitsuyo, and Komatsu Sakyō among others. He is currently a Senior Lecturer in the College of Asia and the Pacific at The Australian National University, Canberra.